"So how's it going?" Dionne asked. "You know, not giving advice, minding your business. Are you doing it?"

"Piece of cake," I said. "Oh, no," I whimpered as Amber hurried toward us, looking like a fugitive from Bide-a-Wee. She was wearing a salt-and-pepper faux-fur parka with long-haired after-ski boots.

Amber did a little twirl. The hair on her boots stood up. "What do you think of the look? Isn't it totally DKNY?"

"More ASPCA," Tai said.

"Like I'd really ask *you*." Amber gave Tai's wrinkled skirt a cold once-over. "Cher, what do you think about silver lipstick with this outfit?"

"Cher doesn't think anymore," De said quickly, grabbing my hand.

"Excuse me?" said Amber. "Does she even talk?"

The blood was pounding in my ears. I could feel makeover fever rising in me. I bit my lip. I cleared my throat.

I was about to break my vow.

Don't miss out on any of Cher's furiously wicked adventures!

CLUELESS
A novel by H. B. Gilmour
Based on the film written and directed by
Amy Heckerling

CLUELESS ™: CHER'S GUIDE TO . . . WHATEVER
By H. B. Gilmour

CLUELESS ™: CHER NEGOTIATES NEW YORK
A novel by Jennifer Baker

CLUELESS ™: AN AMERICAN BETTY IN PARIS
A novel by Randi Reisfeld

CLUELESS ™: ACHIEVING PERSONAL PERFECTION
A novel by H. B. Gilmour

Archway Paperbacks
Published by POCKET BOOKS

Achieving Personal Perfection

A Novel by H.B. Gilmour

AN ARCHWAY PAPERBACK
Published by POCKET BOOKS
New York London Toronto Sydney Tokyo Singapore

AN ARCHWAY PAPERBACK *Original*

An Archway Paperback published by
POCKET BOOKS, a division of Simon & Schuster Inc.
1230 Avenue of the Americas, New York, NY 10020

TM and copyright © 1996 by Paramount Pictures

ISBN: 0-671-56870-1

First Archway Paperback printing April 1996

10 9 8 7 6 5 4 3

AN ARCHWAY PAPERBACK and colophon are registered trademarks of Simon & Schuster Inc.

Printed in the U.S.A.

IL 7+

With thanks to my L.A. homies,
Cameron, Michelle, John, Mickey, Jenny, Rocky,
and the Log Cabin gang,
and the eastern posse, Anne, Evan, and John,
for their valuable assistance.
And for Jessi, as always, with love.

Chapter 1

*C*her, how could you do this to me?" Daddy demanded. He was standing behind his mahogany and leather desk, leafing violently through piles of legal papers. "What were you thinking of?"

Through the French windows of his study, I saw José, our gardener, pruning the hedges around the Calder sculpture. Lawrence, the pool man, was skimming bright pink and purple bougainvillea blossoms off the surface of our swimming pool. And there was Lucy, our maid, waddling from tree to tree, gathering grapefruit and oranges for breakfast. It was a monster Beverly Hills morning. You could hear sprinklers humming on seven-figure lawns throughout the neighborhood.

"Are you listening to me, Cher? I've got a major case coming up, and I was counting on Josh's help.

How could you send him to Seattle at a time like this?"

My dad is fully skilled at cross-examination. He earns about a thousand dollars an hour doing it. So I blinked up at him, put a big smile on my face, and brushed back my long blond hair. Sergio, my colorist, had done way excellent highlights, but now was not the time to admire his artistry.

"Daddy, I was only trying to help," I said.

He fixed me with a withering stare. His bushy black eyebrows knit together tragically. "You were only trying to help? Now, where have I heard that before?" he said sarcastically. Then he turned and with a squeak of his Gucci loafers strode past me out of the room.

"Don't forget to take your vitamins," I called after him. "And you've got a three o'clock appointment with Dr. Bruno, the periodontist. I put his address in your organizer."

I was hurt. Bitterly bummed. Yet I fought to maintain an upbeat attitude. I realized that Daddy missed Josh. I missed him, too. He was my boyfriend, after all. But I wasn't going around like an earthquake took out Rodeo Drive a minute before my custom shirts were ready, was I?

It was true that Josh had left the greater Los Angeles area at my suggestion. It was the only decent thing for him to do. His mom, Gail, was having this deeply dramatic personal crisis in Seattle and totally needed his support. At least I thought so. I mean, if my fourth marriage had hit an oil slick on the matrimonial freeway and was like skidding out of control without brakes, I think I'd want my son nearby.

Josh had tried to convince me that his mom would be fine. "She's been through this before," he said. "My stepdad will say he's moving out, but he'll just book himself into tennis camp for two weeks. Gail will go back to her therapist and support group. In no time, she'll feel strong and deserving again. My stepdad will come home with spin on his serve. They'll make up and be fine. It happens all the time, Cher."

Josh's mom had once been married to my dad. That's how Josh and I met. My friends used to think he was so cute, three years older than us and a real Baldwin. But back then, when I was only ten years old, I did not appreciate Josh. I thought he was a severe pain. He was *sooo* deep and *sooo* caring and always trying to cushion life's blows for me. Which I totally hated. Just because my mom died before I got a chance to say hello to her did not mean I was a shivering orphan in the storm. *Au contraire.* My life has always been way decent. Like having two parents around really guarantees a totally tubular life. Not even!

When Gail and my dad split, Josh moved to Seattle with her. By the time he returned to go to UCLA, we'd both grown up a lot. And all the things that used to annoy us about each other suddenly became . . . I don't know, proper. We fell in love.

So it was easy for me to understand Gail's distress.

"But, Josh, I spoke to her when she phoned here looking for you. She sounded brutally heartbroken," I reminded him. "You've got to go to her, help her through this harsh time."

"Cher, I've got papers due in two courses."

"Excellent," I said. "You can write them in Seattle, away from the distractions of Westwood. I mean, between complaint-rock concerts, movies with subtitles, bookstore browsing, and coffee bars, I don't see how you people get anything done in college anyway."

It took a few days but I finally convinced Josh to board a plane for lumberjack land. We had a totally classic farewell scene at LAX. I mean, my eyes misted over, and I was so grateful that my liner was waterproof. Josh got all choked up, too. "How am I going to get along without you?" he said. "I don't know if I remember how to pick out my own socks anymore."

"Just stay away from the thin navy blue ones. They tend to droop," I reminded him. "And try not to wear flannel *every* day."

Josh laughed. "I didn't get a chance to say goodbye to Mel. He left a message yesterday that he had a big new case coming up. He asked if I'd have time to help him with depositions and other pretrial grunt work. Tell him I'm sorry I can't help out, okay? Explain why I'm going home."

"I will. Will you miss me?" I asked.

"I miss you already," Josh said, leaning down for a goodbye kiss. When we separated, I put a hand on his cheek and tried to memorize his face by Braille. I felt his square, scratchy chin and full, smiling lips. I ran my fingertips through his thick, dark hair and even over his eyelids, which were rimmed with intense black lashes and closed over these amazing Baldwin blues. Finally, Josh adjusted his backpack, kissed the top of my head, and hurried toward the boarding tunnel.

"I'll phone you later," he called over his shoulder. "Tell Mel I'm sorry."

"Don't worry about a thing," I assured him. "Daddy will absolutely understand."

I heard Daddy's Jag tear over the cobblestones of our circular driveway and squeal off toward Century City. Chances were he hadn't taken his vitamins. In fact, I doubted that he'd even drunk the fresh orange juice I'd asked Lucy to fix for him.

"He is so lost without Josh around," I confided to the portrait of Mom, which was hanging in the domed entrance hall outside Daddy's study. She's a down Betty in the painting, young and groovy in full disco gear. Even though I never knew her, I like to pretend she's watching me.

"I feel a little lost, too," I admitted. "But," I quickly assured Mom, "my life is so fun. I'm way popular. And like all these people depend on me. So how can I be lonely, right?"

When I thought about it, it was true. My friends and Daddy, Lucy, and even Josh counted on me extremely. So me feeling lonely was totally whack. And right there I resolved to put aside my petty concerns and do unto others. I'd just put on a happy face and busy myself with good works. I mean, life was huge with possibilities. You never knew when you could do something golden for mankind or who might need a makeover.

As if to prove the point, my beeper went off. "Stay cool, Ma. Gotta split," I said in the seventies-speak I always try to use around her.

I checked the beeper, flipped open my cellular phone, and headed out the door. My Jeep was waiting on the cobblestones. I pointed it toward school, and eager to make a contribution to humanity, I returned Tai's page.

Chapter 2

I'm so bummed. Cher, can you whip around and pick me up on your way to school?" Tai's New York accent crackled through the cellular.

"I'm pulling a U-ey on Sunset this sec. See you in five, girlfriend."

Tai Frazer was my absolutely most challenging makeover. The first time I even saw her, which was her first day at Beverly Hills High School, my heart totally stirred. She was like this neon sign that went, Help, I do not fit in here.

It wasn't just the moving way she'd mumbled incoherently in that random urban dialect. Or the garish punk streaks that sullied her wild and massive hair. She was just shy, awkward, and so ensembly innocent. I remember how I squeezed my best friend Dionne's scrupulously French-manicured hand and said, "De, my mission is clear. That girl is so adorably clueless. We have to adopt her."

Now, way transformed and looking fully like every other desirable Betty in our crowd, Tai was waiting for me. I felt a surge of pride as I spotted her sitting on the rim of the fountain at Wilshire and Santa Monica. Although, as announced, she did look a tad forlorn.

"Dude." Tai boarded the Jeep, slapped me a limp high five, and to my immense relief, buckled up without my even reminding her.

I was trying to stay conscious of vehicular legal nuances like seat belts, full stops, and signaling. I'd been driving totally legally for a couple of months and had already received *two* failure-to-signal citations from detail-obsessed L.A. law officers. Both of whom, I might add, were large, well groomed, and ferociously immune to explanations.

Daddy couldn't believe it. "You were ticketed for a failure-to-signal violation and you couldn't argue your way out of it? What's happening to you, Cher?" he'd demanded. "Where's that little pit-bull negotiator I reared?"

Every time I thought of Daddy now, I felt a furious tug of compassion. Ever since Josh left, Daddy had been frowning a lot, snapping at callers on the phone, grumbling and muttering, and being way demanding.

To the rest of the world, it probably looked like nothing about him had changed. He was just Mel Horowitz, the meanest, most expensive attorney in L.A., the feared Litigator. But I could tell his heart wasn't in it.

"How do I look?" Tai asked, interrupting my

thoughts—which was actually a good thing, since I'd just whizzed through a stop sign and almost clipped this incredibly rude pedestrian. "Do I look like an abandoned geek? Travis won't see me, won't talk to me. Is my face like Zit City? I've been gorging Ring-Dings and Yoo-Hoos for two days."

Travis Birkenstock was Tai's boyfriend. He used to be a total bonehead, one of those guys with baggy shorts, long stringy slacker-type hair, and the easy grin of the mentally challenged. I don't want to sound all judgmental here, but Travis was chronically fried and no respectable girl would actually consider him. Then he met Tai and got into a twelve-step program. Now he's on a spiritual path. His ensembles still leave a lot to be desired, but he's way acceptable and fully into the clarity thing.

"Travis is like slavishly in love with you, Tai. What do you mean, he won't see you?"

"I think it's because he's entered this major skateboard event and he's freakin' over it . . . like practicing all the time. He's into a vicious crisis of confidence."

I hit the brakes. Tai's forward motion was snapped to a halt by the seat belt's stranglehold. "Wow, they work," I said admiringly. "Tai, this is *sooo* dope. This is totally manageable. It's the foremost challenge I've been looking for. When is Travis's event?"

Tai shook a head of lustrous auburn curls—a far cry from the purple-streaked mane that had once screamed *makeover* to me. She looked dazed. "This seat belt's way tight. It nearly cut me in half, Cher. What were you saying about Travis?"

"Just trust me, Tai. When is the event he's practicing for? Do you have a contest flier with you?" I pulled into the school parking lot as Tai rifled through her purse. She handed me the folded flier.

"It's Saturday. Will you come with me?" Tai's big brown eyes were pleading. "Travis is buggin', and I'm practically postal over this myself."

"Doable. Saturday, ten A.M., Venice Skatepark. Count on it, girlfriend," I said.

"Ooooo, Cher!" Tai unbuckled her belt and leaped across the seat to hug me. "You are *soooo* . . ." At a loss for words, she shook her head. "Sooo . . . *you!* I'll call you later, okay? I've got to see Miss Wimmer about my essay on Emily Dickinson."

"How'd you do on it?"

"Sucked air. Totally choked," Tai called over her shoulder. "I defined *recluse* as one who has *clused* again." She shrugged her shoulders, blew me a kiss, and hurried toward the Quad.

My best friend, Dionne, and her significant other, Murray, had just gotten out of his BMW. "Yo, Cher." Murray grinned metallically, flashing a mouthful of gold braces at me. "Wassup, woman?" After beeping his car alarm twice, he turned his baseball cap sideways, and hiked up his baggy designer jeans.

"Girlfriend!" De hugged me, then sniffed the air around me. "Calvin Klein," she guessed. "cK one, eau de toilette for a man or a woman."

I sniffed the air around her. "Body Shop. Leap," I said. We slapped a high five.

"Classic synchronicity." De peered over her sunglasses at my outfit, noting that we both happened to be wearing short-sleeved silk chenille sweaters, plaid micro-mini skirts, and midcalf boots.

"Later, ladies." Murray dipped a shoulder at us and began his practiced hip-hop stroll toward school.

"Wait," I called. "What are you and the Crew doing this Saturday?" The Crew is comprised of what passes at our school for hunks. If you have to date high school boys, the Crew are the only acceptable males on campus.

Elton Lozoff, exceedingly fine looking, whose father is a monster force in the music business, is one of them. I hate to say this, but Elton is massively impressed with himself. It's like he's on ego steroids. The only reason he briefly dated Amber Salk, the flawed queen of big hair, is that she worshiped him. So, naturally, Elton thought she had excellent taste.

And there's Murray, of course, a dean's list student who writes rap songs about the downside of being rich. Murray's dad is a famous Bel-Air cosmetic surgeon. He's rumored to have cloned Janet Jackson from her brother's fingernail scrapings. Sean, Christian, Morrissey, Ben, and Jared are some of the other members.

The female side of the Crew—beyond De, Tai, and me—are Janet; Summer; Alana, whose dad is a renowned TV anchor; Baez, whose mom has been married four times to rock musicians and once to Janet Hong's father; and the previously discussed, coiffurely challenged Amber Salk.

"This weekend?" Murray tugged at his three-carat diamond ear stud. "Nothin' urgent. Yo, why you gotta know?"

"Murray." Dionne rolled her eyes. "We agreed that you would not engage in street slang off school grounds."

"Yo, yo, this is school. What you call this, woman?"

"Don't you *yo* me. This is the parking lot. And don't call me *woman*."

"Excuse me, people," I broke in. "Earth to the Honeymooners. Okay, so you're free this weekend. Excellent. Tai needs our help. Travis is in a skateboard contest and in brutal need of support. I'm putting together a cheering section for him. Murray, pull the Crew together. I want us totally attired. Ultimate gear. We should look our extreme best. De, tear through your wardrobe for something Venice."

"Venice, Italy?" Dionne asked.

"Venice Skatepark," I said, "as in Venice, California."

"You don't mean Geek Beach?"

"That's harsh, De," I said, although everyone knows that Venice Beach is way overburdened with the stylishly impaired. All these zoned-out leftovers of former generations seem drawn to the area. The dress code is like, don't drool and wear shoes indoors.

"Oooo, let me think," De responded. "How about something tie-dyed and a paper cup for spare change?"

"Dionne, our best friend, Tai, needs us. Travis needs us. He's in this major competition, and according to Tai, he's wiggin' over it. We've got to pump him up. Suit up and show up. Saturday, ten A.M. Let's show the world what we—and, by association, Travis Birkenstock—are made of."

* * *

Saturday dawned crisp and almost crud free. By ten o'clock the smog alert had been lifted and there was hardly any haze from Marina Del Rey to Santa Monica. Venice Beach nestled between the two. It was crawling, like literally, with winos. whackos, tourists, and teen castoffs.

De surveyed the crowd, then gave me a major raised eyebrow. "Excuse me. Do you think we may be fanatically overdressed?" she said.

"Dionne, the fact that everyone is pointing and gawking at us doesn't mean *we're* out of place. Our standards are way higher, that's all."

Of course, Amber was the exception. She'd shown up in some silver leather rig with metallic boots and like pretzel braids. Little tourist kids were going, "Ma, look. Princess Leia from *Star Wars.*" But I recognized the outfit from a classic Urban Knights video. It was a cheap bid for Elton's attention.

Naturally, he never even looked at her. He was totally posing in these *GQ* dark glasses and a way decent crumpled white linen Ralph Lauren summer suit—without a shirt.

I thought the rest of our crew looked brutally hot. Christian had his Sinatra straw hat pushed back on his head and a vintage fifties jacket slung over one shoulder. Janet Hong did a *Vogue* thing—stripy skinny midriff sweater over a layered mini that looked like a ballet tutu. Summer wore vinyl capris and these excellent platform sneakers. And, of course, all the girls were waving the cheerleading pom-poms De and I had borrowed from school.

"Maybe the pom-poms are too much." De bit her

lip in an uncharacteristic burst of self-doubt. "I mean, these people are not your basic L.A. Laker celebrity fans. And, Cher, they are staring at us with more than usual slack-jawed awe."

"Dionne, *hello*. We are so not trying to impress this group. We're here to cheer for Travis. And to rampantly support our true blue girlfriend, Tai. Trust me. She'll be way grateful."

I hadn't told Tai I was bringing anyone with me. I'd wanted it to be a big surprise. I was sure she'd be majorly overwhelmed at how supportive the best and the brightest of our school could be.

The skateboard competition was already in progress. I hoped we hadn't missed Travis's moment. I spotted Tai sitting on a beach towel at the front of the contest run. She was craning her neck, looking for me. I waved and caught her eye a split second before Amber shrieked, "Pom-poms, everyone!"

Tai's full lips, which I'd personally taught her to pencil, flew open. Her pale cheeks suddenly flamed with color. I could see in her quickly clouding eyes that something was very wrong. The words "I'm toast" leaped to mind.

Was De right? I wondered. Were we seriously overdressed? Were the pom-poms brutally excessive? Tai was not squealing with delight as I'd expected. Actually, she looked . . . horrified.

I saw all this in an instant, then quickly dismissed it. Tai was a native New Yorker, I reminded myself. They were very high strung. You couldn't always tell what their expressions meant—facial or otherwise. Plus, insecurity is so not my strength.

Amber, Summer, and Baez had begun shaking

their pom-poms and chanting, "Tra-vis! Tra-vis!" while Janet Hong, who'd had Olympic ambitions as a child, somersaulted across the grass. People were like way stunned. Everyone stared at us as we made our way through the extremely casually dressed crowd.

Tai grabbed my arm. There were tears in her eyes. She was speechless—with gratitude, I assumed. I was so moved.

"Isn't this the bomb?" I said, hugging her. "I knew you'd wig, but I didn't expect tears. Everyone's so pumped. We're here to show our support for Travis."

"How could you do this to me?" Tai hissed.

"There he is!" Amber screamed. "Okay, everyone. Let's do it. Who's our hero? Who's our rock? Travis. Travis Birkenstock!"

"This is so incredibly humiliating." Tai's fingernails bit into my biceps. "The skateboard crew'll laugh Travis out of town. Look at them."

I did. They were a truly shabby lot, all in T-shirts and cut-offs—and we are not talking designer grunge here.

"He'll never speak to me again," Tai wailed.

Travis had jumped his board onto a monster slalom run. He was zigzagging through the cones when he heard his name being chanted. He turned to see what was going on. Suddenly a big goofy smile lit his face. He veered off course, the edge of his board kicking two Day-Glo orange cones into the crowd.

"Oh, no!" Tai shrieked, oblivious to Travis's ear-to-ear grin. "Look what you've done. You broke his concentration. He's off the course. He's out of the contest. After all that hard work!"

It was true. Travis was bumping along the grass

now, slaloming through the panicked onlookers. "Far out!" he hollered, pumping his fists in the air as spectators ducked and ran for cover.

"He's our hero. He's our rock. Tra-vis! Tra-vis Birkenstock!" Strangers had begun to take up the cry. Skaters in bikinis and leather-tanned beach bums and kids sitting on their parents' shoulders were chanting along with the Crew.

Tai covered her eyes. "I can't watch. I can't believe you did this. I'll never forgive you, Cher," she shouted. Then she turned and ran blindly through the laughing, cheering crowd.

Chapter 3

*T*he next morning I found myself staring listlessly at the rotating clothes rack in my closet, trying to get a color feel for the day. Everything looked brutally autumn to me, even the pastel shades. I realized I was succumbing to negativity.

I'd been so pumped about coming to Tai's aid. I'd had such excellent expectations. Now I was all like, what went wrong? Which I really hate. I have to say, I felt that Tai had a very low threshold for embarrassment. I thought she'd way overreacted. And I was deeply disappointed that Travis had allowed himself to be so easily distracted. When I have a goal, I'm totally Nike about it. I'm all, just do it.

When the phone rang I hit the speaker button and called, *"Bueno?"*

Josh's cheery voice asked, "How's my girl?"

"Basically," I said, "Daddy is despondent, Tai's not

talking to me, and you're five hundred miles away in the birthplace of environmentally induced depression and Starbucks. Other than that, I'm golden."

He laughed and invited me to unload on him, which I did, striving to crusr. any trace of self-pity—which is so not my emotion. Josh tried to be gentle and tactful in his response, but the word *meddling* did come up.

"I wasn't meddling. I was only trying to help," I protested, pressing the Stop button on the closet rack.

"I know, Cher, but sometimes it's better to let people work things out for themselves."

"Oh, Josh, I miss you," I said.

"I wouldn't be here if you hadn't insisted that I rush to my mom's rescue."

I had pulled two outfits off the rack, a lemony velour ensemble and a short nylon slip dress. I held first one, then the other, against me while I listened to Josh on the speakerphone.

"She's fine, by the way," he said. "Harold, my stepdad, calls her at least once a day. They're going on 'a date' next weekend, a trial reconciliation. But now that I'm up here, I'm probably going to hang for a bit, at least until I finish my lit and poli-sci papers."

I'd just about decided on the slip dress, which would look choice with my urban assault boots, when Josh got to that part about not coming home for a while.

"You were right," he continued. "It's much quieter here. I'm getting a lot done."

I felt like hurling.

It was one thing for Josh to be in Seattle because he

was needed there. It was brutally another for him to elect to stay.

"That's great," I said, with loving but rampantly bogus enthusiasm.

"Okay, I'll talk to you soon. Try to stay out of trouble," Josh said. Then he was gone.

I dressed hurriedly and on my way out of the house punched Dionne's number into my cellular.

"I just got off the phone with Josh. Stress emergency," I confided.

"Mall of your choice, girlfriend," De said. "Beverly Center or Galleria?"

"This is too big for a mall. It's a Rodeo Drive kind of thing. I'll meet you for lattes at the outdoor café on Via Rodeo."

"Rodeo Drive." Dionne was impressed. "You must be desperately bruised."

Dionne was sitting at a petite wrought-iron table under a striped umbrella when I arrived. I couldn't help noticing the Giorgio's shopping bag at her feet.

"Record time," I said, looking over my DKNY wraparounds at the distinctive yellow-and-white bag. "Not only did you get here before me, you've already shopped?"

"Cher, do you think I would trivialize your crisis by boutique-hopping without you? It's an exchange for my mom. I've been totally waiting. What happened?"

"It took me five minutes to drive over and twenty to park."

"I so hate that," De said. "But what happened with Josh?"

I slid into the café chair opposite her. "He's staying

in Seattle. His mom is fine, just like he tried to tell me she'd be. She doesn't need him there, but he's staying."

"Bleak," said De.

"Fully," I agreed. "I am inconsolable. And it's not just me I'm thinking about. Daddy's been deeply torn up about it. He holds me responsible for Josh's leaving."

"Well, you did practically force him to go," De pointed out.

"Dionne," I said, "could you restrain the whipping impulse until I finish?"

The waiter came over. "Two lattes," De said.

"No, this calls for an iced decaf skimmed milk mochaccino and an order of fries."

"Two," De concurred.

"Where was I?" I asked when the waiter left, taking the tasseled, oversize menus with him.

"Your dad," De said. "You were saying how Mel is bummed and blaming you. And how Josh is saying you are responsible for his staying in Seattle. By the way, have you spoken to Tai since the Venice event?"

"I only phoned constantly last night and left multiple messages. According to Amber, who wanted to be the first to confirm it, Tai holds me personally responsible for distracting Travis, getting him disqualified from the contest, and brutally humiliating them both in front of a gazillion badly dressed skateboard enthusiasts. It seems we were too high-profile for the Venice slacker pack."

De fluttered her big black eyelashes at me. "Girl-friend, is there a theme emerging here?"

"What do you mean?" I asked, frantically searching for our waiter and the relief a french fry gorge would bring.

"I mean, maybe you *do* get too involved in other people's problems, Cher."

"That's what Josh was saying, too," I conceded. "But I've been thinking about Daddy. I've been thinking maybe what he needs to get his mind off Josh's being away is—"

"No, Cher," De interrupted. "Don't say it. Don't think it. Don't try it."

"A relationship," I said.

"I knew you were going to say that!" De shook her head. "Cher, you can't play matchmaker for your own father. It's severely personal. Anyway, I think the point we're coming to grips with here is that you should . . . how can I say this delicately . . . like totally mind your own business."

"Way delicate. Thanks, De."

The fries and mochaccinos arrived. I just toyed with my food.

"How come Josh is hanging in Seattle if Gail doesn't need him?" De asked, between fries.

"He says it's a great place to get his schoolwork done."

She almost spewed.

"What?" I demanded as De dabbed her lips with the linen napkin. "You think Josh was lying? You think it's not about college? You think he's mad at me for toying with his life? You think he's found someone up there in save-the-spotted-owl world? As if! De, are you saying that Josh may be revenge dating in Seattle?"

"*I* didn't say any of that," Dionne protested.

"Yet it's tragically evident that's what you meant. You think Josh is like Murray? You think I'm going to find cheap Kmart extensions in the back of his car?"

"Excuse me?" De threw her napkin onto the table. "Girlfriend, you have gone too far," she announced. "I was doing you a total props by not pointing the finger of blame about the Venice Beach fiasco in your extremely vulnerable direction. And here you throw up in my face a painful incident from the historic past. My man furiously assured me that Shawana has never even *seen* the back of his BMW. That polyester braid totally belonged to one of Murray's little sister's friends."

"De, you're holding a lot of tension," I remarked. "I'm going to give you Fabianne's number. She's my masseuse. It'll be so dope. She's got extremely good hands."

De pushed back from the table. "I do not need a massage," she said icily, tossing down a twenty-dollar bill and picking up her shopping bag. "Now, if you'll excuse me, I've got severe business to transact at Giorgio's."

Chapter 4

No amount of fries could release me from my misery. I sat alone at the café, gorging grease for nearly an hour. And viciously obsessing.

There I was, with enough credit cards to outfit a small country, staring blindly across the cobblestone courtyard of a world-class shopping venue, and all I could think of was how I had bitterly trashed those whose lives I'd tried to better.

It was way pathetic.

Now Josh was deserting me. Dionne had dismissed me. Tai despised me. Even Daddy was like terminally grumpy. I kept waiting for someone to yell, "April Fool, Cher! This is so not your life."

I might have been frozen in that Prozac moment forever, but suddenly I spotted a traffic vehicle checking parking meters. I had to go. There was no time to do the credit card thing. I tossed real money at the check and fled.

Running like a casually attired Cinderella toward my Jeep, it hit me. It was what Josh and Dionne and Tai had been trying to tell me all along. The person most brutally in need of my makeover magic was me!

I had to change.

I had to mind my own business.

Whatever it took, I totally needed to avoid suggesting improvements in other people's lives. My days of matchmaking, makeovers, and rescuing were behind me. I took a solemn oath that if by the time I got to my car there was no ticket on the windshield, I would never again meddle in someone else's life.

Tscha! No ticket.

I hurried home, the new me all buckled up for safety and grinding out full stops at the required corners. My gray day was suddenly as bright as a Versace bustier.

There was a limousine cooling at the curb in front of our house. I ran inside, and as if in answer to my prayers, I heard Daddy laughing—for the first time since Josh had left.

"What's happenin', Ma?" I greeted the portrait in the entryway. "Guess what? I'm turning over a new leaf. I'm out of the makeover business. Is that cool, or what?"

I headed down the two plushly carpeted steps to the living room, eager to share Daddy's unexpected but way welcome mood swing.

And there she was, the obvious cause of my dad's sudden giddiness, a stunning brunette suited up in a trim Donna Karan corporate power play coat-dress, Manolo Blahnik heels, and a vintage Louis Vuitton attaché case. She was draped across the white leather sofa in this casually confident way, trailing about a yard of YSL black silk–clad leg.

I was fully impressed.

"Cher, come here. I want you to meet someone," Daddy called cheerfully. "This is Harriet . . . er, I mean, *Ms*. Goddard. Harriet, my daughter, Cher."

"Call me Harriet," she said in a crisp yet sultry voice. "Mel was just telling me that you're interested in film."

"Harriet's a movie producer," my father said, as though he was totally proud of her.

"An independent producer," Harriet corrected Daddy.

You could see that. Everything about her reeked independence. She was flawless. If I hadn't already retired from the makeover game, she'd have been a furiously effective convincer.

"Harriet's got her own production company. They're doing a courtroom drama."

"I'm trying to convince Mel to commit *pro bono* to us on the script. Give it a supportive read-through for accuracy, authenticity, atmosphere. We've got a lowball budget on a high-concept winner here. I can't afford your dad, but I can't afford not to have him either. I need someone with his integrity, talent, and reputation on board."

"I was saying, if Josh were around . . ." Daddy said, with what looked dangerously like the beginning of a frown.

"But this person, this Josh, he's a student, prelaw,

an undergraduate, am I correct?" Harriet Goddard asked, leaning forward with like riveting intensity. "You know the drill, Mel. Never send a boy to do a man's job."

She smiled a mouthful of the most perfect white laminates I'd ever seen at Daddy. They were truly dazzling, framed by full, burgundy Chanel Creme lips.

Daddy grinned, then got adorably self-conscious. "Well, we'll see," he said, shooting me this heart-meltingly modest shrug. He cleared his throat and tried to get all serious again. "It's an interesting idea, Harriet. I just need a couple of days to think it over."

"Of course," Harriet said, in a voice as dark and silky as her tights. She pulled this telephone-directory–size leather notebook out of her Vuitton bag. It had pencil pockets, and credit card and business card holders, and suede divider pages with tabs. She threw the book on the glass table and opened to a big, busy calendar page. "I don't want to pressure you, Mel. That's not the way I work."

She drew a fat gold pen out of its leather pocket and began tapping her perfect teeth with it as she studied her book. "How about next Tuesday? Lunch? Let's pencil it in. I'd like to support a positive decision here. I'm a very nurturing, empowering negotiator— at least that's what my people tell me. I'm proactive and result-oriented, it's true. But my goal is always a win/win setup. Lunch at Granità or cocktails at the Beverly Wilshire? Or is there some other beanery you especially like? I'm open."

My jaw practically dropped. Here was a monster hottie with totally chronic conversational skills. I glanced from Daddy's happy face back to Harriet's, and I was like, go, girl. Harriet Goddard was not your everyday pedicured Betty but a furiously dope babe.

Daddy deserved nothing less.

"And you, Cher." Harriet turned her high beams on me. "If you're really into movies, stop by my office." She handed me her business card. "We're a streamlined but resourceful operation, and I'd be glad to show you around."

"Excellent," I said, and she immediately began leafing through that massive appointment book.

"Let's pencil it in. Okay, I'm jotting it down in my come-up file for follow-through," she said. "So if you don't call me, I'll call you. I think you'll find us interesting."

"Totally," I assured her. "I'm rabidly a movie fan. I mean, not just of the best of my generation, like Keanu and Brad and Leonardo. I even like Mel Gibson and some of the other more mature stars. Like Antonio Banderas. He's old but way righteous. Not like Scott Bakula, who is so last decade. And I have to say, despite all the hype over *Waterworld,* I still think Kevin Costner is pretty random."

"Antonio?" Harriet said. "I'm talking to Antonio's agent on this film. There's something so integrated and principle-centered about the man. He's powerful. Magnetic."

"Fully," I agreed.

Chapter 5

I dialed De's number. "It's Cher. Don't hang up, don't hang up, don't hang up," I urged.

I couldn't wait to tell Dionne and Tai about Harriet Goddard.

The fact that neither of them was talking to me made it awkward. But I couldn't let that deprive me of sharing this way juicy news bite with my very best friends.

I mean, here a monster role model had fallen into my life. A woman of taste, talent, and rampant self-esteem, tricked out in brutally def career couture. A genuine babe who'd made Daddy grin for the first time in weeks. And this was the part I thought would majorly impress Tai and De: I'd had nothing to do with it. I hadn't played matchmaker. I hadn't meddled. I'd just strolled into my own home and there was the solution to Daddy's loneliness all curled up on the wraparound white leather sofa.

Now, cellular in hand, I hurried across my room to catch a last glimpse of her. Harriet had just left the house. From my bedroom window, I could see Daddy dawdling beside her limo.

"Give me three good reasons why I shouldn't hang up on you," Dionne demanded.

"Because I'm completely sorry that I said such a cruel and thoughtless thing to you about Murray."

"That's one," said De.

"Because Ringo Farbstein just gave me the answers to the algebra pop quiz Hanratty's giving your class tomorrow."

"That's two."

I was way impressed with De's coolness. Algebra answers were seriously hard to snag. I'd had to promise Ringo a seat at our lunch table to get these.

"Okay, and three is that I've completely changed. And I can prove it."

"Let me guess: You're shopping the Cheryl Tiegs collection at Sears."

"As if! I mean it, De. You were right about me minding my own business. And I'm doing it. And it's like furiously no problem. I mean, Daddy just met this bitterly serious babe, and he's all happy again and blushing and you know all that cute stuff old people get into."

"And like you didn't have anything to do with it, right?" De said sarcastically.

"Zero, zip, nada, nothing! Her name is Harriet Goddard. She is like the hottest Betty in town—an intimate acquaintance of Antonio Banderas—and she's going to get me into the movie business."

"Antonio Banderas?" De yelped. "Brutally choice. Did you tell Tai yet?"

"I'm speed-dialing the minute we click off."

"Go, girl," De said. "Wait, we can do a three-way. I can conference-call her on Carolina's phone." Carolina is De's mom. She's a totally famous business-person who handles publicity for soap stars, talk-show hosts, and heads of small nations. She's hardly ever home, but she's got these humongous next-generation telephone consoles all over the house that do everything but moisturize and burn calories. "Hang up," De said. "I'll call you back in a sec."

I clicked off my cellular and looked out the window again. Daddy was coming up the drive. There was a bounce to his step once more. I couldn't see his face, but the little bald spot on top of his head looked positively rosy. I was so happy for him. I was like totally kvelling.

My phone beeped, and I clicked it on. "Tai, are you still there?" I heard De ask.

Then there was Tai's voice, kind of small and shy: "Yeah. Ah'm heah."

"Cher?" De said.

"Tai, I'm like utterly abject. I apologize. Please forgive me for, er—"

"Meddling," De prompted.

"Thank you, Dionne," I said coldly. "Tai, I really am sorry that I meddled in your life—"

"She's turned over a new leaf and everything," De interrupted. "Cher's like seriously going to mind her own business from now on. Right, Cher? And she's not going to play matchmaker or force makeovers on tow-ups ever again."

"Dionne, I never *forced* a makeover on anyone."

"What about that woman on the airport bus in New York City?"

"That doesn't count. Her beret was all wrong. And she didn't speak English so I couldn't very well *ask* if she wanted my help, could I?"

"You guys," Tai said, laughing. "You are *soooo* cute. I really missed you. So, you gonna pick me up on the way to school tomorrow or what?"

"Definitely," I said.

"Tell her about who your dad is seeing. You know, and about Antonio," De urged.

"Antonio who?" asked Tai.

"Antonio Banderas," De squealed.

"The elderly hottie from *Desperado?*"

"Yes, and *Assassins*," said De.

"Two thumbs up," Tai cheered. "Wait a minute. I don't get it. Cher's dad is seeing Antonio Banderas?"

"Hello," I shouted, fighting my way back into the conversation. "Remember me?"

"Ooooh, Cher. Ah'm sorry," said Tai.

"Wait, wait, I know," De teased. "That voice . . . It's the all-new, improved Cher Horowitz!"

I toyed with being hurt, but it was so choice to be conversing with my best buds again, to hear Tai's giggle and have Dionne snapping on me, that I burst out laughing instead.

Then, with De's prompting and teasing, I told Tai all about Harriet Goddard and Daddy and about Harriet's invitation to visit her office. I apologized again for distracting Travis from his big skateboard moment. Tai confessed that Travis was really awed by the attention and that he'd had a totally tubular time surfing through the cheering throng.

It was dark outside when we finally got off the phone. "Okay," De said, before signing off, "so tomorrow is the first day of the rest of your reformed life, right, Cher?"

Tai added, "No more makeovers. No more matchmaking. No more meddling. True or false?"

"True, true, true," I vowed. "Trust me, I am *so* over all that."

The test came on Monday. It was a way harsh day. Everywhere I went, people seemed desperately in need of my services.

If Dionne hadn't come over to my house first thing in the morning, I'd have broken my promise by eight A.M., which was when Daddy marched into our kitchen.

He was wearing a red, blue, and green tie that looked like the illustrated encyclopedia of fish. Trout and tuna sailed across the silk between feathery lures and hooks and tackle boxes. It must have been a gift from one of Daddy's clients, a grateful but accessory-challenged outdoorsman.

"Daddy, that tie—" I began.

De winced, then gave me a disappointed look. Here we go again, her hazel eyes flashed.

"What about it?" Daddy grumbled, ignoring his orange juice and going straight for the caffeine kick of Lucy's Spanish-style coffee.

"It's so . . . so fresh," I enthused. "And colorful."

De did a "Whew!" and nodded her approval.

Daddy came to me with his chin lifted so that I could knot the fish tie for him. I did it in desperately controlled silence. I was about to remind him to take his vitamins when he said, "When's Josh coming back? Have you spoken to him lately?"

"He called yesterday morning," I said. "He's going to stay in Seattle until he finishes his term papers."

To my surprise, Daddy took the news with an understanding nod. Then he tore open the packet of vitamins on the kitchen counter. "Well, say hello to him for me next time you speak to him," he said, tossing back the pills with a healthful quantity of fresh OJ. "He's got a good head on his shoulders. And a good heart, too." He kissed my forehead, gave Dionne a wink, and left for work.

"Wow," De said. "What did you do? Your dad's like in a major good mood."

"I know," I said, torn between happiness for my dad and a strange, almost sad feeling. "The thing is, I didn't do anything. I didn't even have to remind him to take his vitamins or drink his juice. De, this leaving people alone . . ."

I didn't know exactly what I wanted to say about it: It works, it's way weird, it makes me feel terminally useless . . .

"Yeah, it's awesome, isn't it?" De finished the sentence for me.

"Brutally," I said.

We drove below Sunset to Tai's house. She was sitting on a bus bench at the corner, waiting for us.

"Dude-ess!" De called to her. "Get on board."

Tai jumped up. The hem of her ankle-length skirt

got caught on the plastic buckle of her high-heeled jellies. She pitched forward, her arms spinning frantically.

"Oh, no!" De yelled.

"Oh, no, is right," I said. "Can you believe it? Two days away from us and she's like totally into retro-wear. Those jellies are so summer of ninety-four."

De shot me an evil look.

"What?" I said defensively. "You call that meddling? You think it's none of my business?"

She nodded.

"Okay, you're right," I confessed. I locked my mouth with an imaginary key and threw it away. "I won't say anything evil about the skirt. Not one word."

Tai managed to remain upright and limped over to the Jeep.

"I know, I know," she said, climbing into the backseat. "This skirt is terrible, right? But I don't have one clean thing left. My mom's like on laundry strike. And everything I own is heaped in a corner of my room."

"The skirt's fine," De said graciously. "Isn't it, Cher?"

"Noble," I said. "Functional but with an edge. And so floral."

Chapter 6

*I*f minding my business had been hard before, school was like an outlet mall of relapse opportunities. Temptation was everywhere. From the moment we parked, putting a barely noticeable dent in Mr. Hall-Geist's rear bumper, the ensembly challenged and socially desperate seemed drawn to me.

Practically the first person we saw crossing the Quad was Ringo Farbstein, the math dweeb. In exchange for the answers to De's algebra quiz, I'd invited him to join us for lunch today. The entire Crew would be there, of course, along with the most desirable babes of Beverly Hills High.

I'd hoped that Ringo would rise to the occasion. But here he was in his everyday high waters, pointy black shoes, and short-sleeved shirt buttoned to the neck.

My fingers twitched with the need to undo that top

button, to tear the plastic pocket protector off the shiny mystery fabric of his shirt. I clutched the strap of my backpack instead and put a cheery smile on my face.

"Hi, hi, hi," Ringo greeted each of us shyly. "Er, you got a minute, Cher?" he asked.

"Of course," I said. "You are lunching with us today, aren't you? I was just going to phone ahead for another place setting at our table."

"Well, that's what I want to talk to you about," Ringo said. "Privately," he added nervously.

"I'll see about the table," De volunteered. She grabbed Tai's hand and pulled her away from us. "We'll see you later, Cher."

"I can't do it," Ringo said when they'd gone. He took a wilted handkerchief out of his back pocket and began furiously cleaning his wire-rimmed glasses.

Without those opticals, Ringo's eyes looked star-tlingly green. His nose looked stronger, too. I caught myself studying him for a moment with new interest. Then I asked, "What can't you do, get the algebra answers?"

"No, I have them. Here." He was about to put his glasses back on. Without thinking, I snatched them from him and held them as he searched through his bookbag. "I mean, I can't have lunch with you," he said, finally handing me the folded sheet of paper he'd been looking for.

"Really? Why not?"

"Because of Janet," Ringo blurted out.

"Janet Hong?"

"She's the best, the bomb. She's like this totally down Betty, plus she's a secret geek, a full-out brain who doesn't flaunt it."

I was shocked. "You mean you're hot for Janet Hong?"

"Hot? I'm ashes, man." He gave me a sad smile. He had way decent lips and classic teeth. "I wouldn't survive a gorge at the same table with her," he continued. "I'd wig, man. I'd go whack, disgrace myself, probably hurl."

"If you opt for the macaroni and cheese, definitely."

Ringo shook his head. A fetching hank of dark hair fell over his mathmeister brow. "I can't do it. So like thanks for the invite, Cher. I hope your friend aces algebra. But I just can't show. Sorry I'm such a . . . you know, dweeb."

My mouth fell open. So did my fingers. Ringo's glasses clattered onto the parking lot tarmac.

He bent to retrieve them about a second after I saw Janet Hong getting out of her car.

"Janet," I hollered, waving wildly.

"Janet?" Ringo looked up.

I stepped on his glasses. "Whoops, my bad," I said, wondering if De would have classified the move as meddling. Not even, I decided defensively. Although, if I were still in matchmaking mode, Ringo and Janet would be a way intriguing possibility. And if I were still all about makeovers, I'd definitely see Ringo as a client for contacts. Without his specs the word *doable* came easily to mind.

Ringo scrambled to his feet. He looked way classier without his unfortunately destroyed glasses. Janet ran up to us. "Dude." She slapped me a limp high five. "Hey, Ringo," she said. "Wow, this is so clean. I was just thinking about you."

"Me?" said Ringo, blinking in her direction, running his hand through his dark, glossy hair.

"You," said Janet. "This minute. I was wondering what you got for that third question on Harding's calculus homework. It's driving me crazy."

"Well, I'm Audi," I said. "Catch you both later . . . at lunch."

I made it to Mr. Hall-Geist's first-period debate class without altering anyone else's life. Which was a massive miracle. There were more bad outfits crossing the Quad that morning than oil-soaked seagulls in Santa Barbara. But I zipped my lip and hurried to class.

Mr. Hall-Geist was taking attendance as I came through the door.

"Elton Lozoff?" he called.

"Here," Elton said.

"Cher Horowitz?"

"Here." I slid into the seat in front of Christian.

Hall-Geist looked at his watch, then at me. "Perilously close to a tardy," he said.

"Mr. Hall-Geist, there was a problem in the parking lot that required my attention."

"Really," he said skeptically.

"Someone rammed your old Mustang. But don't worry, it was on the right side. You know, where the tail light is already broken."

"My tail light isn't broken."

"Well, what do you call it when the red plastic is

like totally cracked and the little lamp is hanging out?" I asked.

Mr. Hall-Geist blinked at me. "Thank you, Cher. Janet Hong?" he called.

"She'll be here soon, Mr. Hall-Geist. She's like into a major calculus crisis."

"Thank you, Cher. Travis Birkenstock?"

There was no answer. Mr. Hall-Geist turned to me.

"Sorry," I said. "Can't help you there."

"Thank you, Cher," he said.

As Mr. Hall-Geist continued taking attendance, Christian passed me two fabric swatches. "Hey, princess. I need an opinion," he whispered. "Which one do you like better?"

"Would my offering an opinion be considered like interfering in your business?"

"Not if I specifically request it. Why, what's shakin'?"

"I am extremely over butting into other people's affairs. Lately, every time I try to help someone, I wind up being hated."

"I could never hate you. Which one do you like?"

I studied the swatches. One was a nubby tangerine weave; the other was a mustard-colored faux leather.

"Are you upholstering a dentist's office?"

"No, I was thinking of having a dinner jacket made," Christian hissed. "And I hate you."

"No, you don't," I said. "You love me, Christian. And I'm really going to miss you."

Christian's parents were divorced. According to the terms of their totally insensitive joint-custody agreement, my best boy pal was heading east to Chicago to spend second semester with his mom.

"Sorry I'm late." Travis skidded through the door, then kicked up his skateboard and caught it under his arm. "I had my watch on upside down."

"Take your seat, Mr. Birkenstock." Mr. Hall-Geist was sitting at the edge of his desk. "All right, let's get started. Elton Lozoff?" he called.

"Here," Elton said again.

"Yes, thank you, Mr. Lozoff. It's time for you to present your argument. Let's see . . ." Mr. Hall-Geist read from a piece of paper on his desk. "'Are Foo Fighters a Ripoff of Nirvana?' Elton, I believe you're arguing the pro side of the issue."

As Elton slowly stood up, the Persian Mafia, led by the darkly handsome and furiously financial Paroudasm Banafshein, began to snicker and hoot.

"Quiet, quiet," Mr. Hall-Geist admonished them. "Mr. Banafshein, you'll have your chance to counter Mr. Lozoff's arguments in a moment."

"Yeah," Elton said, "that's what democracy is all about, Parou. Everybody gets to have an opinion— even people like you who've never even been to a Nirvana concert or personally met Dave Grohl or even listened to the Afghan Whigs. I mean, do you even know who my father is? Only like one of the top guys in the music business, and I had the first Foo Fighters CD off the line, so really what would I know about music, right?"

About half the kids in the room applauded. Travis held up a piece of paper with a big 9.5 scrawled on it.

Paroudasm stood up, twirling the keys to his BMW. "If I go home tonight and ask it of my father, tomorrow morning he will own not just the company for which your father works, but the land on which its corporate headquarters is situated."

Now the cheers came from Parou's corner at the back of the room.

"The Boo Radleys played at my bar mitzvah," Elton shouted. "It was at the Hollywood Bowl."

"My father owns the Hollywood Bowl," Paroudasm shot back.

I raised my hand.

"Yes, Cher?" Mr. Hall-Geist said.

"My beeper just went off, Mr. Hall-Geist, and I'd like to be excused, please."

"No."

I stood up. "But it's from my friend Tai Frazer, and it must be brutally important. She never calls during class time."

"It'll have to wait, Cher."

"Tell her hi for me," Travis hollered.

"Me, too," said Baez. "Oh, and find out, did she bring back my quilted purse? I mean, she borrowed it last week, okay?"

"She's got two of my CDs," said Elton. "Let's see . . ." He pulled a banded group of index cards out of his pocket and rifled through them. "Yeah, here it is. Siouxsie and the Banshees and Hootie and the Blowfish. I want them back."

Paroudasm said, "My father owns Hootie and the Blowfish."

"Mr. Hall-Geist," I protested. "I just want to say—"

"Go, Cher. Leave. Thank you for attending class today. Goodbye," said Mr. Hall-Geist.

I punched in Tai's number the minute I hit the hall.

"Do you have an extra gym suit in your locker?" she asked. "I couldn't find mine this morning. And anyway, it's so rancid it can practically stand on its own. I mean it was all I could do to snag this skirt out of my mom's hamper."

"Thank you so much for helping me check my gag reflex, Tai. It's working. Where are you?"

"De and I are heading for the Quad."

I looked out the door. "Okay, I see you both. I'm on my way," I said.

My beeper went off again. This time it was De. I called her back.

"So how's it going?" she asked as I came down the steps toward them.

"How's what going?"

"You know, not giving advice, minding your own business. Are you doing it?"

We were face-to-face now. I clicked shut my cellular and shrugged. "Piece of cake," I said.

"Oh, no, here comes Amber." Tai threw her hands over my eyes. "Don't look, Cher."

"Why? What's she wearing?"

"A dead German shepherd, I think. At least I hope it's dead," said De.

"Tai, I can handle this," I said, peeling her fingers off my face.

"You are so wrong," said De.

"Oh, no," I whimpered as Amber hurried toward us looking like a fugitive from Bide-a-Wee.

She was wearing a salt-and-pepper faux-fur parka with silver raw silk leggings and long-haired after-ski boots. Her own hair had been teased—*taunted* was probably closer to the truth—into a huge dark mane.

"Are you guys blowing off PE again?" she said.

"No, we're on our way to Stoegerville," De assured her, Ms. Stoeger being the name of our ferociously athletic phys ed teacher. "We just have to snag a gym suit for Tai."

"I'd lend you one"—Amber looked down her surgically altered nose at Tai—"but mine are so petite." She did a little twirl. The hair on her boots stood up. "What do you think of the look? Isn't it totally DKNY?"

"More ASPCA," Tai said.

"Like I'd really ask *you*." Amber gave Tai's wrinkled skirt a cold once-over. "Cher, what do you think about silver lipstick with this outfit?"

"Cher doesn't think anymore," De said quickly, grabbing my hand.

"Excuse me?" said Amber. "Does she even talk?"

The blood was pounding in my ears. She needs me, she needs me, she needs me, it seemed to say. It was always a brutal challenge to run into Amber and not suggest improvements. Her attitude invariably reeked. And today's kennel costume, coupled with that snotty comment and the fact that poppy seeds from her morning bagel were dotting her teeth, reduced the chances of my remaining silent from slim to none.

Suddenly the buzzer sounded, and kids started pouring out onto the Quad. It was time to change classes.

Amber was waiting for me to say something. I bit

my lip. I cleared my throat. De shot me a warning look. Tai's face crinkled in alarm. I could feel makeover fever rising in me. I had to get rid of Amber or I'd break my vow.

That was when I spotted Elton crossing the Quad. He was smiling contentedly, completely absorbed in rifling through his CD collection. I was desperate. "Look, Amber. There's Elton," I blurted out, "and so alone."

"Elton? Alone?" She spun on her hairy heels to see for herself. "I'm Audi," she called, hurrying across the grass toward him. "Cover for me with Stoeger. I'm not doing PE today."

De and Tai gave me these grave looks as we headed for the gym.

"That was cheap," De mumbled. "I expected more of you."

Tai shook her head, clearly disappointed.

Hello, I responded. "Merely commenting on the presence of a Crew member crossing the Quad does not constitute matchmaking."

There was this tense silence. Then the three of us burst out laughing. We shrieked and jumped and slapped high fives and barely regained our composure before PE.

Chapter 7

Minding my own business was way exhausting. By the time Thursday rolled around, I'd earned my French manicure and Swedish massage. Thank goodness Fabianne, my masseuse, made house calls. I was in no condition to drive. In fact, on my way home from school that afternoon I'd been pulled over by a member of the LAPD.

"Do you know how fast you were going?" he asked me.

"Do you know that a mustache would draw attention away from your weak chin?" I almost said. But that would have been who knows how many points off my license. So I stifled it, went all wide eyed and teary, and avoided the ticket.

But the stress was beginning to show. In four days—not even counting Amber—I had passed up three excellent matchmaking opportunities and turned away more makeover candidates than the Estée Lauder counter at Saks on a rainy Saturday. I should have been celebrating my success; instead I felt burnt out, cranky, useless.

The fact that I hadn't heard from Josh since Sunday did not help.

Fabianne was kneading my back with her warm oily hands when the phone rang. My heart leaped. "Maybe it's Josh," I said, punching the speakerphone.

"Cher Horowitz?" a crisp, businesslike voice said. "Hold please for Harriet Goddard."

After a few bars of mellow Beatles music, Harriet was on the line. "Cher, I'm so glad I reached you," she said silkily. "I just left your dad. What a paradigm of integrity that man is. He's got an inner directedness and unique contribution capacity that mirrors my own deepest values."

"Daddy's fully decent," I agreed.

"Absolutely," said Harriet. "And I consider it a genuine achievement to have him aboard. We just closed favorably on a consultant package. And now I'm trying to tie up some loose ends on the deal. I saw on my meeting notes that we discussed your stopping by GP—"

"GP?" I said, absentmindedly. Really, I was trying to assess what Daddy's new working relationship with Harriet meant. Was he gone on the girl? Did he need my help?

Harriet was the most furiously self-assured babe I'd ever seen Daddy with. Besides myself, of course. I mean, one of my former stepmothers was practically bionic. She'd had everything lifted but her IQ. And although she was a shark in the real estate market,

Josh's mom, Gail, had major flake tendencies in matters of the heart. Then there was Mom. From what I'd heard, she was a soft touch for everything. A bell-bottomed, fringe-jacketed do-gooder—which is where, Daddy says, I inherited my desire to better people.

Maybe Daddy's taste had changed. Maybe strong, independent hotties like Harriet were the wave of the future around our house. It could not be considered meddling, I decided, to find out more about the girl—just in case.

"GP. That's Goddard Productions," she was explaining. "Are you still interested in stopping by? I told Mel I was going to give you a call. I'm absolutely obsessive about follow-up. Without it, there's no commitment, no process for viable trust-based relationships."

"I so agree," I said. "Follow-up is fully golden. Pencil me in."

She did her throaty chuckle. "Okay, I've got my book open," she said. "How are you tomorrow at two-thirty? Are you free?"

"Er, I've got history."

"Who hasn't?" said Harriet.

"I mean, I'm in school at two-thirty. Ms. Geist-Hall's history class."

"A conflict. Well, conflict resolution is one of my strengths. Let's see . . ." I could hear the gold pen tapping against those big perfect teeth. "Got it," she said quickly. "I'm tied up after two-thirty. But I could have Brad show you around."

"Brad?"

"Bradley Dietz. You've probably heard of him.

Terribly today. Sensitive but consequential. Young. He's one of our most bankable new directors. AFI out of NYU."

NYU, I knew from my trip to the Apple, was New York University, home of the more educated hackeysack players of Washington Square Park. "AFI?" I asked.

"American Film Institute, sweetie. Where Danny DeVito directed his first flick. But Brad's already shown at Telluride and Sundance. It's a perfect brainstorm. Bradley Dietz is *the* person to introduce you to Goddard Productions. Perfect, perfect. He interned here. And he owes me. At least that's what he told thousands of film buffs when he accepted that award last summer. Cher, I'll have my assistant set it up, and we'll get right back to you."

"Okay. Thanks," I said. But Harriet had already hung up.

I glanced over my shoulder at Fabianne. She'd heard the entire conversation.

"That was Harriet Goddard," I explained. "She's like Planet Hollywood with great legs. She's way impressed with Daddy. He told her that I'm a movie fan, so now she wants to show me around, you know. She's an independent film producer. That's how they talk."

"Your back is tight," Fabianne said. "When was the last time you spoke to Josh?"

"Is it that obvious?" I asked.

"Wild guess," said Fabianne, walking her thumbs up my back. "Why don't you give him a call before your spinal fluid dries up and your vertebrae turn to chalk."

I waited until Fabianne had gone before phoning Seattle. Josh's mom answered on the fourth ring. If a *hello* could sound desperate, Gail's did.

"Hi, Gail, it's Cher," I said with an upbeat attitude. "How are you?"

It was the wrong question. Too hard. Gail took a couple of stabs at an answer, but it sounded as if she was only guessing. "Er, fine? Um, I'm . . . well, really, I'm . . . It's stopped raining."

"Are you all right, Gail?"

Stumped again. "Me?" she said.

Clearly, I'd caught her in the middle of a flake attack. "You sound kind of . . . preoccupied." I liked that word so much better than *postal* or *out of it*.

Gail liked the word, too. "Preoccupied. Yes," she said, brightening a bit. "I am. A little. Preoccupied."

"Gail, is Josh around?"

"No," she said.

"Is he like at the library, all working hard on those papers?"

"What papers?" Gail asked.

My heart clanked against my dry ribs. "You know, the ones he has to do for school."

"School?" said Gail.

"Do you know when he'll be back?"

"No," she said. Then, "Oh, wait. The library. Yes. Yes, Cher. That's where he is. I think that's what he said. Oh, dear, I was up all last night. I'm just in a fog today. I'm sorry, Cher. Do you want me to give Josh a message?"

"No," I said. "That's okay. Just tell him I called."

I felt a lot worse when I hung up. Josh had said his mom was fine. Well, Gail didn't sound fine to me. She sounded nervous, anxious, and unsure of herself. She sounded like she didn't know whether she was *supposed* to tell me where Josh was.

I could practically feel my spinal fluid curdling. I couldn't call Fabianne again. I couldn't call my buddy Christian either. A victim of cruel joint custody, at this very moment he was winging his way to the Windy City to spend six dismal months with his mom. And I didn't feel like shopping. So I just let my revolving clothes rack spin and pulled out the first outfit that caught my eye, this totally bleak vinyl suspender skirt and skinny ribbed sweater. Then I headed downstairs for a mood-altering food fest.

I was in the kitchen with Lucy when Daddy came home.

We were pigging out big time. I had a heifer-size helping of nonfat frozen yogurt in front of me, and Lucy was sucking down last week's leftover Chinese takeout. She was so concerned about me. I could tell by the way she kept sighing between heaping mouthfuls of moo-shu chicken.

Lucy is our housekeeper and my domestic best friend. She's a little older than my dad and twice as wide. And she's got this furiously neurotic fixation that if Daddy notices her she'll be fired. So the minute Lucy heard the front door slam, she threw down her chopsticks and skittered out of the kitchen.

"Cher!" Daddy bellowed.

"In here, Daddy," I called.

He poked his head into the kitchen. "Who was that big woman in the black uniform who just ran into the broom closet?"

"Probably Lucy," I said. "She's cleaning the house."

"Starting with the refrigerator?" he asked, eyeing the profusion of takeout containers on the kitchen counter. "Did Harriet Goddard get in touch with you today?"

"Yes, Daddy."

"Good. I agreed to look over that script of hers. She's a very persuasive woman," Daddy said admiringly. "A black belt negotiator. Single-minded, self-centered. Knows how to get what she wants."

"She's way attractive. And a choice conversationalist," I said, pausing for Daddy's reaction.

He just nodded and started out of the room. Then he turned back. "Are you okay? You look a little—"

I gave him a great big smile. I hate to worry Daddy about anything. He gets all serious and involved, which is so hazardous to his health. Anyway, what was I going to say? I mean, he'd just recently gotten over missing Josh and being all mad at me about it, so I certainly didn't want to bring Josh's name into the discussion. And it would have been totally bowhead to ask, can minding your own business cause depression? So I flashed him a bright dental reassurance and said, "I'm at peak performance, Daddy. Totally classic."

"Okay. Just checking," he said. Then he winked at me and headed across the hall to his office.

I waited until I heard him close the door, then I went to the broom closet and let Lucy out.

Chapter 8

At 10:45 A.M. on Friday, just as Travis took the podium to debate the validity of comic books as art, my beeper went off.

Mr. Hall-Geist's cute shiny head swiveled in my direction. He crossed his tweed-jacketed arms so you could see the frayed elbow patches and waited patiently while I tried to identify the caller's number. He smiled knowingly when I raised my hand.

"Emergency?" he asked.

I stood up. "Well, I don't actually know," I confessed. "It probably is because I don't recognize this number, except it's a Valley exchange. I mean, it's not my father. He's over in Century City, and anyway, I certainly know his number. It could just be one of those pesky long-distance companies. I mean, it could be MCI or Murphy Brown for Sprint. They always call at the most inconvenient times."

Mr. Hall-Geist was nodding and nodding. Finally, he interrupted me. "Thank you, Cher. You may go."

"Thanks, Mr. Hall-Geist," I said. "And, Travis, I just want to say that while I personally would never compare Marvin the Martian with Picasso's *Guernica,* I definitely respect your right to do so."

Most of the class applauded me. Amber, of course, fanned her face with her notebook as though she'd smelled something rank. I could care less. I was Audi.

In the hall I clicked open my cellular and dialed the mystery caller. "Goddard Productions," someone said.

"Hello, this is Cher Horowitz. I'm returning a page."

There was a brief interlude of boring lite music again, then a deep and languorous, "Hello, Cher? Brad Dietz here." The voice was the masculine match of Harriet Goddard's—self-assured yet laid back, crisp but friendly. "Harriet's told me all about you. I'd be delighted to show you around Goddard Productions. Are you free any time today?"

I thought about it. "I always do lunch at the Quad so that wouldn't work. I guess I could blow off PE," I said. "Ms. Stoeger sprained her ankle so it'll just be this substitute who's such a cadet she wears a whistle on a lanyard. I mean, when was the last time you ever saw a lanyard, right? In like summer camp maybe? But I'd have to be back for history at two anyway, so that's not a great idea either—"

"After school, then?"

"Doable."

"Great. I'll pick you up—"

"I've got my Jeep. Ooo, and I have to give Tai a lift.

I promised. So why don't you just give me the address and I'll check it out in my Thomas's and be there around four."

"Four is perfect," Brad said. He gave me the address, which I wrote down, and then he started to give me directions and I stopped writing.

People in L.A. always give you directions. And they're always saying, you take the freeway and get off at this exit and all, as if it were no big thing. Right, like let's play bumper tag at eighty miles an hour with really angry military aircraft workers who've recently lost their jobs due to congressional budget cuts and short, depressed retired people who mix up their medications and can't see over the steering wheel.

That's why I have a Thomas Guide in my Jeep. So I can get places without ever going on the freeway. Once was enough, thank you.

Lunchtime, our regular table at the Quad was packed. De and Tai each scooched over to make room for me. I shimmied in between them and set down my Diet Snapple and smoked turkey croissant.

In addition to Travis, who'd been making guest appearances at the table ever since Tai returned from New York, Ringo Farbstein had become a fixture. He and Janet Hong were this week's Extra item—with no help from me, of course. Although, happily, Ringo had not replaced the eyeglasses I had stomped, and he looked so def. Across the table from me, Janet and he were making small talk, getting all misty-eyed over sines and cosines.

To Janet's right, Elton was filling out his CD-of-themonth-club coupon, oblivious to the white angora fluff Amber's sweater was leaving on his dark shirt-sleeve. Since the day I'd sent her scurrying across the Quad to alleviate his loneliness, the big-haired one had gone Velcro over Elton again. Now she was hanging on to his arm and trying to chow down a lethal bowl of cafeteria chili at the same time.

Next to Amber, Murray was jotting notes for a new rap tune. I could see his mouth working as he silently sounded out the words. "Yo, yo, Dionne," he asked suddenly. "What rhymes with *BMW?*"

De thought about it. "Bubble you," she said.

"Bubble you? That's the best you can come up with? *Bubble you?*"

"Well, it rhymes," De snapped.

Travis leaned across Tai. "Hey, Murray, man, how 'bout *trouble you?*"

"*Trouble you?*" Murray thought about it, then shook his head. "What's wrong with you, Travis? How am I gonna work *trouble you* into an urban anthem?"

Travis shrugged. "You know, like, I hate to trouble you but get your butt off my BMW?"

"Phat," said De.

"My man!" Murray leaped up and leaned over the table to slap Travis a high five.

"No, *my* man," said Tai, cuddling closer to the now-beaming bard of the boardies.

My croissant tasted bitterly reconstituted, like turkey-flavored cardboard. A quick attendance-taking around the table revealed that I was the sole solo. Even the birds and squirrels circling the lunch court seemed to be paired off today.

To make matters worse, De suddenly turned to me and asked, "So what's the news from Seattle, girlfriend? When's that college man of yours coming back?"

I shrugged and made a big deal of letting De know my mouth was full and that I couldn't speak. I patted my lips with a paper napkin and chewed the pasty-tasting sandwich.

"You don't know?" De asked.

"He didn't call?" Tai chimed in.

"He must've called," De said. "I mean since Sunday morning, right?"

"Sunday morning? That's nearly a week ago." Tai was shocked.

"Well, she could have called him," De said.

"Yeah, I guess. Cher, why didn't you call him?" Tai asked.

I chewed and chewed and blotted my lips.

"Wassup?" Murray said. "Who's not calling who?"

"Josh is in Seattle, and he hasn't called Cher for nearly a week," Tai said.

"Get outta town," said Travis. "How come?"

Everyone was looking at me now. Their expressions ranged from curiosity to concern.

I swallowed and took a sip of Snapple to wash away the last vestige of indigestible poultry and pastry. If there's anything more sickening than school cafeteria food, it's having your friends feel sorry for you. I totally hate that.

"Cher, are you all right?" Tai asked gently.

I so wasn't. I found the sudden surge of public pity bitterly humiliating. "Sure, but I won't be able to drop you off after school," I found myself saying. I gave Tai the big carefree grin that worked so well with Daddy. "I'm really sorry, but I've got a date with one of today's most bankable young directors. Brad Dietz. He's AFI out of NYU. You know, sensitive but consequential. And young."

Tai's mouth fell open. "Cher, you're not going to two-time Josh, are you?"

I flung back my long, highlighted hair, which must have looked awesome in the dappled sunlight that filtered through the lunch court's palm trees. "Not exactly," I said, picking up my tray.

"Is he seeing someone else? Is Josh Jeepin' on you?" De demanded.

"You've got a date with Brad Pitt?" Travis said. "I mean, even I know that dude. He's like a movie star."

I felt extremely bummed, but I locked my jaws around that bogus grin like a pit bull. "Excuse me, please. I've got to change for PE," I said, and left the table as quickly and gracefully as I could.

Wallowing in misery is so not my thing. Phys ed was just what I needed to cut through my morbid mood. I mean, generally, I'm not all that into it. I do my aerobics and step work at home, and I've got a choice trainer at the gym. But halfway through class, I had this total revelation about Josh. Basically it was like: been there, done that, what's next?

I was stretched out on the bleachers, soaking up some rays, when I remembered how tortured I'd been in New York City about why Josh wasn't answering my pages. Then there was the international incident when Josh was in Paris. I'd been jealous, thought he was Jeepin' on me, jumped to all sorts of smoked-out conclusions. Each time there'd been a deeply plausible explanation for it all. Now it was *déjà vu* all over again.

Next to being pitied by my friends, I hate being neurotically insecure. It's so demeaning. So I sat up, dusted off my gym suit, and decided to trust Josh and move on with my life—which did not include joining the volleyball game in progress.

Chapter 9

*T*he address Brad Dietz had given me had a low-end zip code. What a blow. Goddard Productions was located on the lot of a movie studio in Burbank. Which meant the Valley. Which, in terms of taste, meant *don't even bother.*

With nothing but raw guts and a Thomas Guide, I drove all the way from Beverly Hills to Burbank alone. It wasn't like I was expecting a T-shirt or bumper sticker commemorating the event, but it was a big deal to me. Particularly since I had to navigate through the burnt grass and mini-mall capital of the world without setting tires on a dreaded L.A. freeway.

It took me a little longer than I'd thought. I arrived in Burbank half an hour late.

Things started to look up at the studio gates. There was a guardhouse at the entrance, and a uniformed employee actually found my name on his clipboard and said, "Go right on through, Miss Horowitz, you're expected."

I pulled into this busy little sun-drenched world of mustard-colored stucco buildings and followed the guard's directions to a long row of bungalows, one of which had a plaque on it that said Goddard Productions.

I don't know what I was expecting. I mean, the place looked nothing like Harriet Goddard. She knew how to dress. This little kind of wooden trailer that housed her company didn't. Oh, there were nice touches here and there: a trendy cactus, an ancient leather sofa on which a colorful Santa Fe–style blanket had been tossed, a big old scrubbed-oak rolltop desk outfitted with a computer terminal. But Goddard Productions was basically one big room divided into a reception area and about three little cubicles.

In the reception area, a Betty who looked only a year or two older than me was watering a geranium. She was wearing the twin of my cinnamon sweater, only hers was pale pink, which looked extremely dope with her choppy-cut wild auburn hair. "Hi, can I help you?" she asked. She had friendly green eyes and zero attitude.

"I'm Cher Horowitz," I said. "Excellent sweater. Chronic yet comfortable."

"Totally," she agreed. "That color really smokes with that blond thing you've got going. I'm Lauren Roberts, film student and indispensable office gofer. You're here to see Brad, right? He's waiting for you. Last cubby on the left."

She pointed me in the right direction, and I thanked her.

If Lauren hadn't said it was Brad in there, I'd have thought I'd walked in on the Banderas man himself. He was perched at the edge of a large, cluttered desk. There was a telephone pressed to his ear, and he was peering out the window through vertical blinds as he nodded and listened. Even with his back to me I knew he was a Baldwin and a half.

He had black, shoulder-length hair pulled back in a neat ponytail, and his jaw, like the rest of his form, was way forceful.

I cleared my throat and knocked on the frosted-glass cubicle wall.

Brad didn't turn. He just put up his hand, index finger pointed, asking me to wait. I had time to study the loose lines of his Armani jacket and to notice that the linen-draped leg swinging off the end of the desk ended in a Gucci loafer with no sock.

"Done," he said, hanging up the phone and turning toward me. "Cher?" he asked, lowering his head and staring at me over the tops of his ultra-dark glasses.

I nodded. "And you're Brad, right?"

He had that hot Banderas stubble on his cheeks and chin. And one of those brutally beautiful Val Kilmer noses. That was the good news.

The bad news was that Brad Dietz was in accessory overload. My eyes kind of pinballed from the glint of his single gold earring to the gold chain around his neck to the skinny hammered gold bracelet that shared a wrist with his underwater, three time zones, gold Rolex. And then of course there were those signature Gucci stirrups on his shoes, just above his tanned but naked ankles.

I have to tell the truth here: I don't think he was wild for my attire either. While I was studying Brad, he was definitely giving me the once-over. Then all of a sudden, he hopped off the desk, made a picture frame of his hands, and watched me through it.

"It's a director thing," he explained. "Sweater?" he asked, squinting through his fingers at my cinnamon cashmere and lamb's wool blend.

"Gap," I replied.

"Skirt?" He made a gesture indicating that I should turn.

I twirled for him. "Faux leopard. Ungaro."

"Jacket?"

"Calvin, of course."

"Shoes?"

"Spectator with ankle strap by Chinese Laundry."

"It's a look. It speaks," Brad said.

"Really? What does it say?"

"Young."

That was funny, because I was thinking that Brad dressed old. "Whatever," I said, making the W sign. I mean, underneath those *GQ* whiskers, *L'Uomo* threads, and QVC jewelry, he was just your basic twentysomething.

"Whatever?" Brad laughed and copied the sign. "I love it."

He came toward me now with both hands extended. "Harriet said you were attractive but, man, she didn't say star quality. You really are a knockout. Have you ever acted?" He grasped my hands and sort of shook them both at the same time. "I know I'm freakin' you, right? I talk too much. I'm like totally intense. But I'm sensitive, too. Believe me."

"Oh, I do," I said, taking back my hands.

Brad looked at his watch. "Listen, Cher, I thought I'd take you around to some of the sound stages. They shoot lots of stuff here, features and TV. But it's getting kind of late. And I was also going to show you some of our post-production rooms—you know, editing, sound, like that. And I've got a wall of scripts here that you could look over. The problem is I've got a meeting in Century City in less than an hour."

"That's okay," I said. "We can do this some other time."

"Excellent. How's eight tonight?" Brad asked. "There's a big opening in Westwood. Should be an interesting flick. I'm on the list. After the Century City sitdown, I'll hit my place for a shower, then pick you up. You're in Beverly Hills, right? Brainstorm. What do you say? I promised Harriet I'd give you an intro to the biz. This'll be perfect. Perfect."

It wasn't like I had to check my book or anything. My social life was brutally lite. And anyway, it was just a Friday night movie in Westwood. Sort of.

Except there'd be giant klieg lights outside the theater and velvet ropes holding back hordes of fans. And *Entertainment Tonight* and *Extra* trolling for sound bites. And flashbulbs popping and paparazzi being punched by irate New York actors. And me on the arm of a sensitive yet consequential director.

"Excellent," I said. "What's the dress code?"

"Well, it's a small but serious film. Italian director. Subtitles, I hope. I hate dubbing. Lots of heavy hitters jetting west for the occasion. Scorsese, De Niro, Pesci. I'd dress dark. Dark and, you know, deep."

There were five messages on my answering machine when I got home.

I pressed Play, then slipped out of my jacket and skirt. The first call was from De, wanting to know whether I'd turned off my cellular. I ran to my backpack and got out the phone. Right. I had hit the Off button by mistake. I turned it back on and tossed my sweater onto the four-poster.

The next two messages were from De and Tai together, courtesy of Carolina's conference-call option. "Hello. Girlfriend, where are you?" De asked.

"Cher, it's me, Tai. Are you okay? You were like so spaced at lunch. It was that turkey, right? Fully rancid. Plus way too much mayo."

"Cher, I know Josh is not Jeepin' on you," De cut in. "I'm like rampantly sorry I even mentioned the possibility. He's as t.b. as they come. Totally true blue. And so are you. You're not really going out with that other guy—"

"Who is he, anyway?" Tai wanted to know. "And what does *bankable* mean? I said it's like a bank shot when you play pool, right? But De thinks it's financial, like in savings bank."

I was smiling by then. It felt so good to have my friends calling me, even if they were acting all worried about my welfare. Every once in a while I forget how popular I am and suspect that I've turned into a Moe. I revved up the volume on the answering machine so that I could hear it from the bathroom. Then I turned on the shower and made a mental note to ask Daddy what *bankable* meant.

De and Tai kept going for a while. Finally De said, "We're going to the movies tonight in Westwood. Or maybe Santa Monica. Want to come?" Then both of them shouted, "Call us!" and hung up. I heard the beep. Then nothing for a sec. Then, tscha, there it was!

". . . Boy, do I miss you. I'm sorry I haven't called. Things have gotten a little crazy here. The papers are coming along okay, but Mom's . . . Well, I'll tell you when I see you. But she just told me that you called yesterday."

I splashed out of the shower, wrapped myself in plush pink terrycloth, and ran back to the bedroom. Josh! I wanted to hug that fully noble compact Panasonic message taker to my wet and soapy heart. That voice, that tender, sincere, totally Josh sound, was way comforting and warmer than my robe.

". . . I thought you'd be home from school by now. I wish you were. How's Mel doing? Mom just walked in. We're going away for the weekend. She says hello, says tell Mel hi, too. Listen, Cher, I'll call you the minute we get back to Seattle. Okay. Gotta go. Love you."

I wanted to play back Josh's message, but right after the beep came Daddy's voice and it was mad. "Cher, where are you? I've been paging you for an hour and you haven't called back."

"Whoops, sorry, Daddy," I told the machine. "My cellular was off."

". . . I'm leaving the office right now. I'll be out for

dinner but home by midnight. And I expect you to be there when I get in, young lady."

Midnight. Hit a celebrity-packed opening in Westwood at eight. Movie, two hours, max. Cup of coffee after the show. Maybe ask Brad what *bankable* means. Home by eleven forty-five. Achievable, I decided. Running my French-manicured fingers through my wet hair, I hurried back into the bathroom for my squiggly rollers and clarifying lotion.

I was blow-drying and thinking about all the good things I'd be able to tell Josh when I spoke to him— like how I'd sworn off makeovers and matchmaking and was learning to mind my own business just as he'd always said I should—when a harsh question came to mind. Was it two-timing for me to attend a Hollywood event with a slightly older man who I'd met a mere two hours ago? I mean, was this the kind of date where Brad Dietz was just keeping his promise to Harriet Goddard who'd promised to introduce me to the movie business, or was this a date-date?

The phone rang. I shut off the dryer and picked up the bathroom extension. *"Bueno,"* I said.

"'*Bueno*'? What is *that*? Cher?" said Brad. "I'm going to pick you up at seven-thirty. What's your address?"

"You won't believe this," I said. "I was just thinking about you."

"Why wouldn't I believe it? I'm egotistical, arrogant, self-absorbed."

I laughed.

"No, really," he said. "Didn't you notice that? Most

66

people do. Of course, I'm sensitive, too. But enough about me; what were *you* thinking about me?"

"How sensitive are you?" I asked.

"Not all that much."

"Proper. Here's the thing: I've got a boyfriend. And I really want to go to this opening with you, but not if this is a date-date, you know?"

Brad Dietz laughed. "I'm flattered, but my heart is otherwise engaged."

"You're not married, are you?"

"Nope. Get dressed. It's almost seven. And what's your address?"

Chapter 10

*T*he front door chimes clanged at seven thirty-five. "Sorry I'm late," Brad said. There was a white limo waiting behind him. "Never mind, Ben," he told the uniformed driver who was coming around the front of the car to open the door for me. "I've got it."

Brad helped me in. "Okay, Ben, let's go," he said.

The backseat was dove gray and had miles of leg room, plus a tiny TV, a minibar stocked with Diet Coke and Evian, and a single red rose sitting in this adorable, built-in vase. It also had a CD player. Brad began shuffling through a selection of disks.

"Chronic wheels," I said, running my hand over the plush upholstery. "When Harriet stopped by the other day she was in a burgundy town car. It matched her outfit—Donna Karan with Yves Saint Laurent stockings. She's furiously stylish and so coordinated."

There was no reason I couldn't while away some drive time learning more about Harriet—for Daddy's sake, of course.

"Harriet's a trip," Brad agreed. "Savvy, single-minded, self-assured. She's totally focused."

"Definitely. But what does she do? I mean, what does a producer do?"

"Depends. Some producers just bankroll a project. Raise or invest the money to get a movie going," Brad said, pulling a CD out of the pile. "Some line up the money and the talent. Some, like Harriet, get involved in everything, from figuring out how much making the movie will cost, and finding the best screenwriter for the project, to casting the principal roles and nailing down a director. Harriet is an indie."

He glanced at me. "An *independent* producer," he explained. "She'll develop a package—budget, script, and talent—then sell it to a studio to be made."

"Righteous," I said. "And she's way attractive. She must have a gazillion boyfriends."

Brad shrugged. "I've never seen her with a man she wasn't doing business with."

"Not even!" I exclaimed. It sounded like Harriet was a love indie, too. At least Brad Dietz didn't know of any special someones in her busy life. Tscha. That cleared the field for Daddy. "I mean, she's such a brutally classic babe. Totally awesome."

"Awesome?" Brad laughed. "That's Harriet. She's got a million projects and proposals and packages in development at studios all over town."

"Like when does she even have time to shop?"

"No wasted energy. She focuses on what's most important to her all the time. Harriet is a producer whose most important, successful, and creative project is herself," he said. "Me, I'm a director. I'm always looking for a new project to work on."

I should have paid more attention to that last remark, but I was still thinking about Harriet Goddard. She didn't waste time and energy trying to fix other people. Her mission in life was achieving personal perfection.

"You're saying she's like a perfectionist, right?" I said to Brad.

"Not *like*. She is." He pulled out a second CD. "What's your pleasure?" he asked. "I've got the new Philip Glass opera based on Sinatra's Hoboken years or Pavarotti sings Richard Penniman's greatest hits."

"Whatever," I said.

"I love that." Brad made the W sign. "Whatever. It's so, you know . . . young."

The music was way severe. I couldn't even imagine the video. Fortunately, Brad lowered it after a minute. "How do I look?" he asked, opening his arms to give me an unobstructed view.

His black hair was still in a ponytail, and his stubble had been neatly trimmed.

I did *my* director thing. I made a telescope of my hands and squinted at him through it.

He had replaced his everyday gold hoop with a diamond stud, I noticed. The gold chain and bracelet were gone, but he'd added this humongous blue sapphire pinkie ring. And he was wearing a long white silk scarf, a wide-shouldered, loosely fitting, deep gray suit, a black collarless shirt, and black slippers.

"Suit?" I asked.

"Claude Montana, Neiman-Marcus."

"Shirt?"

"D&G silk. Two years old. Steven Seigal collection."

"Shoes?"

"Cesare Paciotti. Velvet."

"Socks?" I asked. It was a joke. He was sockless again.

"Cute," he said. "You hate it, right?"

My heart started to thump. My palms got sweaty. I could hear Dionne's voice in my ear. This is a total mind-your-own-business opportunity, it said. Tai's voice followed: Cher, you promised. No more makeovers! Then I thought, what would Harriet Goddard say? Nurturing? Empowering? Proactive?

"It's so . . . win/win," I finally decided.

"Win/win?"

"Totally," I told Brad, and we both started laughing.

"Now me," I said.

Brad stopped laughing. "Cher, I'm a director. I'm very opinionated. Very assertive," he warned.

"My dress is too short?" It was a sleek black mini-slip.

He nodded sadly. "Great gams, though. Seriously invigorating legs, and the shoes . . ."

"Charles Jourdan."

"Brainstorm," said Brad.

"Blouse?" I asked hopefully. I was wearing a viciously dazzling sleeveless see-through over the tight spaghetti-strap slip. Josh loved it. De had been

71

pressuring me for the brand name and place of purchase for two months. I planned to surprise her with it for her birthday.

"Too young," Brad said.

"I *am* young," I pointed out.

He reached over and removed my absolutely most cherished sequined headband. I felt my carefully coiffed locks flop forward.

"Better." He pulled a hard leather eyeglass case out of his breast pocket. "Try these," he said, handing the case to me. I snapped it open and recognized the tortoise-trimmed black shades inside from a wicked two-page spread in the current Italian *Vogue*.

"But it's nighttime," I protested.

"Trust me. The lights outside the theater will be blinding. You won't be the only one in dark glasses, but you'll be the only one in those. And the earrings, Cher . . ."

I grabbed my earlobes. "What?" I asked.

Brad shook his head. "Frivolous," he said. "A darker lipstick could have taken the edge off. That pale pink is so . . . fifties. What are you doing tomorrow? I may be free. There's a savvy boutique on Rodeo that Harriet loves. It's got serious transformational attire. Let's check it out."

I could feel my face growing hot. I was seconds away from a massive hive attack. That was all I needed now: young, frivolous, and a face full of zits. I put on the trendy black specs and shrank back against the Ultrasuede.

I couldn't believe what was happening. Brad Dietz

had found a new project to work on. He was doing a makeover on *me!*

I saw the arc lights cutting through the ozone layer before we even turned the corner. They were mounted on a monster flatbed truck parked just outside the movie house. The street was so bright, it could have been daytime. And it was crawling with limos, black, white, and burgundy. Ours joined the line inching forward.

One by one, the big cars stopped in front of the theater. As their passengers stepped out, flashbulbs would go off like fireworks on the Fourth of July, and you'd hear the crowd go, "Ooooo," or "Ahhhh," or, if it was no one special, there'd be like this "Ugh" and then a disappointed grumble.

I have to say, after Brad's severe assessment of my costume, I wasn't as totally pumped with confidence as I could have been. In fact, I felt a flutter of apprehension as our driver, Ben, pulled closer to the marquee. I mean, maybe Brad was a consequential, bankable young director and all, but without my sequined headband and wearing the wrong lipstick, really, who was I? My popularity was in serious question here, and, face it, my public recognition factor was way low.

Harriet Goddard would know what to do in a situation like this, I thought. But, of course, Harriet wouldn't *be* in a situation like this, not in radically retro lipstick.

Suddenly we were at the entrance to the theater. Brad hopped out of the car, then turned to offer me his hand. I was so glad he'd given me those glasses to hide behind. I smoothed down my too-short dress and put one invigorating leg after the other onto the red-carpeted sidewalk.

And a cheer went up. "Cher! Cher! Ohmigod, it's her!"

Flashbulbs started to pop. Even with Brad's glasses on, they were blinding. "Yo, yo, Cher! Over here!" a familiar voice boomed.

Murray? I thought.

Brad had my elbow and was hurrying me forward, into the theater.

"I can't believe it. I'm gonna die! It's her. Cher! Cher!"

It was Tai.

"Oooo, I'm kvelling." Dionne shrieked. "Cher. You go, girl!"

"Rock on!" Travis hollered.

I waved and blew kisses in the direction of their shouts. I was way moved that my homies had chosen Westwood over Santa Monica.

As I stepped inside the theater, another familiar voice rang out.

"Cher? What are you doing here? And why didn't you return my call, young lady?"

I whipped off Brad's shades and ran right into Daddy's arms.

After I explained the cellular mishap and introduced Brad to Daddy, I noticed that Harriet Goddard, in this shimmering ankle-length gold Moschino, was nearby. She was chatting up three chalk-striped designer suits, who were massively engrossed in what she had to say.

"Perfect, perfect." Harriet's fully focused voice cut

through the drone of greetings around us. "A scarcity mentality is unacceptable in today's market," she was saying. "You don't want to entrust a project like this to people who have a difficult time sharing recognition, power, or profit."

She was all business and beautiful. Savvy and centered. Single-minded and self-assured. I loved the way she sounded. Her language, like her rich brown hair and deep burgundy lipstick, was totally today.

Then she saw Brad and me. She gave her rapt listeners a gracious smile and excused herself. And when she came over to us and took Daddy's arm, I noticed how he was beaming at her.

Maybe Brad was right, I found myself musing. Maybe my look was too young, even passé. I'd always prided myself on being brutally now. But I was High School. Harriet was Hollywood.

I checked out Daddy's gaze again. It looked way worshipful to me. It looked like he might be thinking what I was thinking: Harriet Goddard didn't just say, Perfect, perfect. She was.

"Brad," I murmured as the four of us walked down the aisle of the theater to the seats reserved under Harriet's name. "I'm not all that deeply committed tomorrow. If you still want to, we could spend an empowering hour browsing that boutique Harriet loves."

"You want me to go shopping with you?"

"Brainstorm," I said.

Brad reached into his pocket and pulled out a wallet-size electronic organizer. He clicked it on and checked his appointments. "Viable," he decided.

"Perfect, perfect," I said.

Chapter 11

*S*o long, cute. Hello, savvy.

I was way psyched on Saturday. It was time to take action. Make some strategic choices. And what better way to begin than with a power shopping spree? Brad and I met early for a cappuccino and planning session. Then it was like, whip out the plastic and go for the gold!

Harriet's favorite boutique turned out to be a total upper-management mecca. In addition to executive hottie wear, it catered to the makeup and accessory needs of Hollywood's female power players.

With two thumbs up from Brad, I invested in a horde of junior exec outfits. They were big-shouldered, swagger-and-attitude suits in serious colors. The skirts were way longer than what I was used to. Practically knee-length. But I was no stranger to sacrifice. At Brad's suggestion, I deposited my pink satin mini chemise in a boutique bag and slipped into a righteous, burnt sienna herringbone.

In my action-oriented new suit, I perched on a stool at the makeup counter and let a sophisticated older woman revise my colors.

I didn't mind the smudgy charcoal eyeliner or the cocoa buff cheekbone-enhancing contour blush, but the forty-five-dollar burgundy lip creme that looked so proactive on Harriet turned Halloween purple on me.

Brad thought it was dramatic, theatrical. I thought so, too, in a kind of *Nightmare on Elm Street* way. The cosmetician clinched the deal.

"It's assertive, yes," she declared, "but savvy, sophisticated, self-assured."

I glanced at Brad. He nodded. "I'll take two," I said.

In my burnt brown suit and assertive face, we hit Yves Saint Laurent for stockings and Gucci for a leather engagement book. I also snagged a pair of towering strappy Manolo Blahnik shoes, some empowering clunky jewelry, a DKNY mock croc shoulder bag, and sundry goods from Escada, Prada, and Bruno Magli.

Our last stop on Rodeo was the optical shop where Brad had acquired his dark Italian specs. I tossed away my scarcity mentality and purchased a personal pair. Then I saw the best accessory ever. A way proper pair of clear, nonprescription glasses that made me look not just confident but totally ready to take a meeting and talk high concept.

It was time to go deeper.

I asked Brad to recommend some important business videos, books on tape, and even reading material. Improving your vocabulary is an excellent make-over option. Doing something good for humanity is choice, too. But first things first. We were off to Brad's favorite humongous book boutique. Escalating past the espresso bar, we headed directly to the management/career/business books section.

I was browsing through an illustration-free text on principles of management, when suddenly Brad started to vibrate. I mean, one minute he was jotting down a reading list for me and the next he was tugging at the collar of his black turtleneck, adjusting his gold chain, and fiddling with his earring.

"What's up?" I asked.

"Lauren Roberts," Brad said, jamming his fidgety hands into the pockets of his fawn suede jacket and pointing with his bristly macho chin.

I looked down the aisle. Sure enough, there was the good-natured, green-eyed Betty from Goddard Productions. I couldn't believe it. She was wearing the exact same shoes I'd changed out of half an hour before. And her headband in her auburn hair was just like the one Brad had plucked from my head last night. Only without sequins. She had excellent taste, I thought. Even if it was on the young edge.

"Lauren," I called.

Brad gave me a desperate look.

"What?" I asked.

"Never mind," he mumbled as Lauren saw us and headed over.

"Hi," she said. "Cher Horowitz, right?" She made a move to extend her hand, then laughed at herself as she realized her arms were filled with books. "I'm sorry. What a jerk, right? I wasn't even sure it was you. Wow, you look supremely snazzy. And I love those glasses. They're much healthier than contacts, and they look excellent on you."

"Thanks," I said. "It's like a new look."

"Smokin'," she said, then turned to Brad and gave him a big happy smile. "Hey, you're up early. And in a bookstore. Not my fantasy of how you'd spend your weekend. But you're looking totally . . . Brad."

"Thanks. I think," he said. He was twiddling the earring again. "Let me guess—film books, right?"

Lauren shrugged. "A girl's got to do what a girl's got to do," she said, "especially if she wants to get ahead in the rough-and-tumble world of cinema. Hey, I'm not going to be a Goddard gofer forever."

Now Brad laughed. "I'd be surprised if you stayed past your internship. Lauren's working at GP as part of her film school program," he explained. "She wants to be an editor."

"I've already cut three student films," Lauren told me. "Got paid for one of them, too. I guess that makes me an amateur professional. Hey, nice bumping into you guys. See you, Brad." And off she went—taking Brad's attention with her.

"So which do you recommend?" I asked him. "This two-thousand-page management epic without a single picture, or the leadership, teamwork, and motivation book—which at least has arrows, triangles, and charts?"

No response. I coughed. *"Hello.* Is there a Bradley Dietz at home?"

He kind of blinked me back into focus. "She's a nice kid," he said. "Okay, what's the question?"

We decided against both books and picked up

Daily Variety, The Hollywood Reporter, and two instructional audiotapes instead. One was about highly effective people, and the other was about thriving on chaos. I also got *Stop Aging Now* and *Your Food Personality Plan.* Self-improvement does not begin and end with management skills.

I listened to the audios on my StairMaster. One of them had these little musical interludes between chapters, but it was hard to get a good step rhythm going. So I took a proactive approach. I turned on MTV at the same time. It was a down move. Brutally effective. The tapes offered choice lessons in personal change.

Of course, I had to stop about every five minutes to either answer the phone, look things up, or add new words to my Ask Brad vocabulary list.

By Sunday afternoon I'd already learned about half a dozen chronic words. My favorites were *viable,* which the dictionary said meant "capable of sustaining life" but could also mean "workable." And *multitasking,* which was doing more than one thing at a time.

I'd also spoken to De and Tai several times, Janet Hong twice—but only because Ringo beeped her in the middle of our first conversation—and Summer, Baez, and Elton once each. Also, Christian called from Chicago. He said it was just to find out whether I was *absolutely certain* the fabric swatches he'd shown me were tacky. Then, before I could respond, he said he'd really only called to say he missed me and that he'd buzz me again soon.

And I had filled a whole page of one of Daddy's legal pads with such dynamic, empowering, and mysterious phrases as "free-floating empathy," "lobbying clout," "turnaround options," "sitcom syndie sales," and "pilot commitments."

I loved the sound of the new words I was learning. I recited them in the mirror. I sang them in my post-aerobics shower. I tried out a couple on Lucy.

"Lucy," I said, as she chopped vegetables at our kitchen work station, "tonight I'm lobbying for stir-fried instead of boiled veggies. I'd like you to embrace my judgment here and overcome a deeply embedded habit to cultivate a higher, more effective one."

She threw down her knife and stormed out of the kitchen.

Shortly after dinner I phoned Brad. I had my vocabulary list in hand. We had scarcely discussed the first two phrases when he got another call. "Cher, it's Harriet," he said when he got back on the line. "I'll call you back in five, okay?"

"Viable," I responded.

I decided to turn the interruption into a multi-tasking opportunity. So while I waited for Brad to get back to me, I started to assemble my wardrobe for school.

The phone rang again. I hit the speaker button. "Brad, give me your input on this. Which do you think best reflects a confident yet inner-directed team player? The beige Dolce and Gabbana suit or the menswear fabric Prada?"

"Brad? Who's Brad?" Josh asked.

I was so glad to hear his voice. I could hardly wait to tell him about my evolutionary growth. How transformational and effective my new focus was turning out to be. I mean, as I had heard on a tape only that afternoon, I was living the principles. Focusing on myself. No longer trying to build my emotional life on other people's weaknesses.

"What does that mean?" he said.

"It means I'm changing, Josh. I'm no longer an ingenue on the big screen of life. *Ingenue* means like a furiously powerless Betty," I explained.

"I know what *ingenue* means," Josh barked.

"Excuse me? I don't want to be negative here, but you sound really reactive. Which is not the principle-centered approach for solving professional *or* personal problems. In fact, it's the total opposite of pro-active, which is a far more nurturing and viable option."

"Cher, I've had a very rough weekend with Mom. I'm very tired, but I wanted to check in with you. Find out how you're doing."

"Which is what I'm trying to tell you, Josh. And I know you'll be way proud of me because I am *so* over wasting my time and energy on others. I'm starring in my own drama now. Taking myself seriously. Thriving on chaos. Finding a way to win."

"Who is Brad?" Josh asked again.

"He's a consequential yet sensitive young director whose work has already been shown at Telluride and Sundance. And he's helping me with my vocabulary list and many other value-driven changes."

There was a click on the line. "Josh, hold on a sec. That's probably Brad," I said.

"Great. You give him my value-driven, proactive best, okay?"

I punched Call Waiting. "Brad?" I said.

There was another click.

"Yeah, it's me. Is that your other line?" Brad asked.

"No," I said.

Josh had hung up.

Chapter 12

Monday I picked up Tai on the way to school.

"Ohmigod, Cher," she gasped. "What happened to your mouth? Did you like have an allergic reaction to something? Your lips are all purple. Your whole face is like different."

"It's my new look," I said. "And my mouth is not purple, it's burgundy buff. Get in and put on your seat belt."

"Wow, check you out," Tai said, buckling up. "Those glasses are way decent. And the outfit. Frantically hot. What are you being?"

"Savvy, inner-directed, self-assured. It's like executive star style," I told her. "I feel it actualizes my internal maturity and emotional strength."

"Brutally," she agreed. "It totally actualizes you. Cher, can I ask you something?"

"Of course," I said. "We're members of a complementary team."

"Do you think I'm too fat? I mean, I've been grazing Häagen-Dazs like a certified heifer. Ben and Jerry are like my new best friends."

"Tai, you're the creator. You are in charge."

"Of what?"

"Of your own body image. I mean, what I think isn't the point. I'd like to empower you here. I want to nurture your fragile self-sufficiency and urge you to reflect on some positive options. Tai, you don't want the only vision you have of yourself to come from the current social paradigm—or the opinions and perceptions of the people around you, do you?"

"Not even!" she asserted. Then she thought about it. "Well, it depends," she said.

"On what?"

"What's a paradigm?"

"It's like a model or a pattern."

"I guess not then," Tai decided.

"Duh. Then don't ask me if you're fat. Think for yourself. Make yourself your own most important, successful, and creative project. That's what I'm trying to do."

De was waiting for us at our usual table in the Quad. She was emptying a packet of forty-calorie sugar-free cocoa into a cup of hot water as we walked over. Travis was there, too, waiting for Tai.

In a teeny-tiny leather skirt and bare-midriff sweater, De looked fiercely foxy. Though young. She glanced up at me from under a hot red beret that perfectly matched her lipstick. Her double-lashed hazel eyes blinked in shock. "Cher. Your face," she said.

"You been sucking on a ballpoint pen?" Travis asked. "That happens to me all the time. Like I forget I'm chewing on this pen, and the next thing you know my lips are all blue . . . or even purple once, like yours."

"Thank you for sharing that, Travis. No, I have not been sucking on a pen."

"It's Cher's new look," Tai volunteered. "Burgundy buff lipstick like all the paradigms wear. Right, Cher?"

"Paradigm is not that kind of model, Tai." I spun for De, who had taken a sip of cocoa. "It's like executive chic," I explained. "A take-charge kind of look. You know, strong, self-assured, savvy—"

"Oh, like Cruella DeVille?" Travis ventured.

De laughed. Cocoa exploded from her nose.

"Very attractive, De. Thank you for that wet and wild accolade."

De clapped a napkin over her lips. Then helpful Travis smacked her on the back. De started coughing and choking.

I jumped back, but it was too late. "You spit cocoa all over my new suit," I said. "De, how could you? It's a Prada."

"The shoes are cool, too," Tai said. "Record setting. They're definitely the tallest I've ever seen at this school."

Just then Murray hip-hopped over to the table practically tripping on his baggy jeans. "Woman, your face is a mess," he said.

"She choked on her cocoa," Tai explained.

"Naw, I mean Cher," said Murray. "And those threads. Wassup with that? You look like Dionne's mama after her Oprah makeover. I mean, Carolina is slick, but she's old."

"Mature," De corrected him.

"Whatever," said Murray. "Why you wanna wear them strappy, second-story shoes?"

"Excuse me. Are you the official representative of *People* magazine's best and worst dressed issue or is this just a freelance dis?" I asked. "I hardly think you're in a position to criticize cutting-edge exec wear, Murray. Given your draggy baggies, oversize Eddie Bauer flannels, and backward baseball cap. Which is all *so* two years ago."

"Oooooo," said a couple of kids who'd overheard the exchange.

"Cher, you may be my best friend," De growled suddenly, "but don't be bad-mouthing my man."

"Tell her!" There was a mini crowd gathering.

"That is bitterly co-dependent, Dionne. And anyway, I didn't trash your Galleria schoolgirl ensemble. Cocoa on a Prada is so not fixable."

"Aw, Cher. She didn't mean it," Tai said. "She just choked."

"Tai, she choked laughing at me. I mean, given the chance to evaluate my new look, my so-called best friend spewed!"

Tai hung her head. De looked way hurt. Even Murray appeared to be upset. "What Cher fails to understand," he was explaining to Travis, "is that my attire, like my street slang, is a conscious expression of peer group solidarity and is not influenced by arbitrary fashion commands issued by out-of-touch senior citizens in Paris or New York City."

"Wow," Travis said.

Had I been too harsh? It was true that I hadn't been operating from my higher self. I hadn't listened to my friends with true patience, openness, and the desire to understand. Now I desperately wanted to say or do something to make them feel better.

But that would be way wrong. I was committed to change. I was not in the rescue business anymore. I was no longer trying to build my self-esteem on other people's weaknesses.

"Excuse me," I said. "First-period chemistry calls." And I turned on my ruthlessly statuesque Manolos and headed off to class.

Chapter 13

*G*rowth is a lonely business. My beeper didn't go off once all day. My cellular stayed tucked away in my DKNY mock croc shoulder bag. Even Mr. Hall-Geist was surprised. When a pager beeped in the middle of Summer's debate, Mr. Hall-Geist didn't even turn around. He just said, "No, Cher. You may not be excused."

It was so humiliating. Everybody knows I'm the one who always gets beeped because I'm way popular. But it was Elton's beeper, and I had to sit there while he told that to Mr. Hall-Geist in front of the entire class.

I skipped lunch. I had no desire to confront the Crew again. And anyway, I'd had a heifer-size portion of Special K for breakfast. Additional calories might endanger the slick fit of my unappreciated but excellent, slightly soiled suit. Instead, I sat on a bench under a tree and popped an inspirational audiotape into my Walkman.

The tape was all meditations and affirmations for getting ahead in corporate life. I followed the instructions and did the breathing exercises. Then I started reciting the affirmations. "I am enough. I will survive the merger. I am in charge. I will survive the cutbacks. I am a winner. I won't be downsized."

Instead of making me feel peaceful and confident, the tape made me brutally queasy. The background music was all like synthesizer flourishes with waterfall and lapping wave interludes. After about five minutes of listening to it, you needed a seasickness pill to keep from hurling.

I was *so* not centered.

I put away my Walkman and meditation tape and pulled out my new soft leather Gucci appointment book. Like Harriet Goddard's, it had pockets for everything from pens to credit cards. Mindlessly seeking comfort, I ran my fingers across the embossed face of my gold Amex. But not even the feel of a major piece of plastic purchasing power could lift the harsh funk into which I was tumbling.

All afternoon I struggled to stay on purpose, to focus my higher self on higher education. But I couldn't concentrate in class.

I kept wanting to phone De, but then I'd get all, well, she was the one who laughed at me.

Then I'd think about calling Tai and practically heave, remembering how I'd lectured her on self-sufficiency.

Worst of all, I'd start missing Josh and replaying last night's bitter rebuff.

Josh, my evolved, compassionate, flannel-wearing Baldwin of a boyfriend, had hung up on me. Disconnected. Which was a brutally major dis. But for some reason I couldn't work up a righteous rage about it. All I could think of were my own defects of character.

It was like I hadn't even given Josh the gift of good listening—which every book on tape I'd read over the weekend said was totally mandatory for a principle-centered person. I'd barely given him the space to say he was tired. I'd massively ignored the fact that he'd had a rough weekend. I'd been so single-mindedly focused on my big transformation that I never even asked Josh how *he* was.

I felt awful. Not in charge. Not even Cher.

And by fifth period my calves ached and I had these major blisters on my ankles from hiking up and down stairs in my savvy, strappy new shoes.

Daddy was in his study when I got home. He had a desk full of work in front of him. He hardly looked up as I passed his door. It seemed like since I'd given up reminding him to take his vitamins and had stopped reviewing his daily ensembles, we didn't have much to say to each other.

I noticed how disheveled his hair was. He'd been running his fingers through it again, maybe even tugging at the thinning, dark curls. Daddy did that when he was troubled or frustrated. And of course he was squinting at the yellow legal pad before him.

"Daddy," I began. I was going to suggest that he put on his reading glasses. Then I bit my faded burgundy lip. Giving advice implied superiority, I reminded myself, and it also robbed the recipient of creative self-sufficiency.

Daddy looked up. "Hi, honey. You're home early. Don't you usually meet Dionne after tennis on Mondays?"

"Sometimes," I said.

"When did you say Josh was coming back? I could really use a hand with these briefs." Daddy threw down the pad and shook his head. "Logan's down with a cold and some of the other clerks who usually help out are working on Sy Rapaport's case this week."

"Josh wasn't all that specific," I said. "But I could help out." There was a golden idea: I'd make a contribution. Lose myself laboring alongside Daddy. Hang in the study with him and do something useful.

"No, not now," he cut me off abruptly. "This one's too complicated. I haven't got time to explain it." He looked at his watch. "Harriet's picking me up in a couple of hours. There's some big testimonial dinner she thinks I should go to. So, was there something you wanted?"

"No, Daddy, that's okay." I waggled my fingers at him and started to walk away.

"Cher," he called after me.

"Yes, Daddy?" I turned with an eager smile. He did need me after all.

"Are you limping?"

"New shoes," I said. I could feel my smile slipping.

Daddy nodded abruptly, then picked up the legal pad again. "Why are you dressed like that anyway? Are you in a school play?"

The phone rang. I checked my purse. Daddy opened his desk drawer. We both pulled out our cellulars.

"Mine," Daddy said, waving the card-thin black slimline. "See you later, honey."

I went up to my room and studied for a while. My phone rang twice all night, and each time my heart quickened with positive expectation. The first call was a wrong number. The second was Amber, wanting to know if I had Elton's new beeper number. I didn't, but with Amber on his trail, I could figure out why he'd gotten a new one.

At around seven I heard the doorbell ring. I went out into the hall and from the top of the stairs saw Daddy hurrying out of his study to greet Harriet, who'd let herself in.

Daddy had changed into the dark pinstriped suit I'd picked out for him less than a year ago. It was way elegant. But the checked shirt he was wearing with it was totally wrong. He was knotting his necktie, grumbling about how he could never get it right.

Harriet laughed and poufed out the matching silk handkerchief in his breast pocket. She was in a slinky sequined number with a long skirt slit up to her thigh. Just looking at her shoes made me wince. They were even taller than my Manolos.

"Mel, that shirt is divine. Perfect, perfect for a casual, corduroy kind of evening. But a Sulka or something Paul Stuart, preferably blue, would be so much more effective." She looked up at me. "Hi, Cher," she called cheerily. "Don't you agree?"

"Brainstorm," I said. But what I thought didn't seem to matter. Daddy hadn't even argued with her.

He was already on his way upstairs to change. "I'll be right down," he called to Harriet. "Grab yourself a drink."

He winked at me in passing. I did the dental thing. But something inside me felt crushingly bruised. Daddy didn't need me for anything anymore.

I mean, Harriet had fully righteous taste. Her suggestion was excellently correct. And I had sworn off giving unsolicited fashion tips, even in the privacy of my own home. So it should have been like totally no big deal. Still, I had this sense of how last year's Miss America would feel as she passed that tacky crown to this year's winner.

That was Monday. Things went downhill from there. Josh didn't phone that night or the next. De and I were politely avoiding each other. Tai seemed to be practicing the self-sufficiency I'd preached. She fully stopped sharing her problems with me. Daddy was furiously focused on the new case. His eating habits took a dive. Telltale takeout containers from low-end drive-throughs began to litter his desk.

The only high point in an otherwise desolate time was a surprise call from Christian. It was Wednesday night. I was at home bettering myself. After rinsing Lucy's outstanding but caloric dressing off a petite mesclun salad, I'd had a light dinner alone. I was curled up in the den, paging through recent business book purchases, when the phone rang.

"Girlfriend, talk to me," Christian's cheery voice commanded. "I am utterly blown away to find you at home. I just took a wild chance and punched your number. I never really expected to achieve contact with the social queen of West Coast teendom."

"Christian! Oh, it's majorly hot to hear your voice." I tossed down the book I was browsing. It knocked over my neatly stacked pile of affirmation audios. I didn't even care. "I mean, it's like way win/win," I squealed. "Totally one of those spontaneous events that explodes, you know, experiential barriers beyond like mundane expectations. Oooo, boyfriend, I have been missing you!"

"I know *exactly* what you mean—I think. Now, tell Christian everything. How are you and those golden homies, De and Tai?"

"Oh, excellent . . . I guess."

"You guess? Okay, moving right along . . . What are you doing tonight?"

"Just putting in some quality time on self-improvement," I said.

"Excuse me? What's to improve?"

"Oh, Christian, you are so . . . empowering and nurturing."

"And cute. Don't forget cute."

"And cute," I said. "The total cutest. And bright and sensitive. So I know you'll understand. I've had a great awakening. It's kind of involved, but in essence I'm through helping others, particularly those deeply scripted in scarcity or what some people call 'the zero-sum paradigm of life.' Isn't that the bomb?"

"I'm speechless."

"I'm no longer building my emotional life on other people's weaknesses, Christian. You know, no more offering advice, doing makeovers, pairing off people who don't even have a clue how perfect they are for each other."

"Why not?" Christian asked. "It's what you're good at."

"But it's a viciously other-directed mentality. And so time-consuming. I believe my efforts are better spent focusing on achieving personal perfection."

"And that's why you're home alone tonight—and don't know what's up with your best buddies De and Tai?"

"Basically," I admitted.

"Cher, listen to me. There's nothing wrong with helping other people. And you have this completely unique, totally endearing talent for it. You just can't *force* it on anyone. You have to wait until they ask for help. You know, like I did when I asked your opinion about those two swatches."

"Are you still mad at me because I hated them both?"

"Never, Cher. I respect you. I respect your opinion. I love your taste and style. That's why I asked you. And then I did what I wanted anyway."

"Oh, no, Christian, you didn't!" I said, scrunching up my nose at the thought. "You had a dinner jacket made of that pimply orange weave?"

"Of course not." Christian cackled happily. "I had one made of the yellow leather—and it's chronic, golden, totally classic. It's a full-out conversation piece. Like walking into a party wearing a ripe banana."

"So much for my advice." I laughed. Then I filled Christian in on the premiere I'd gone to with Brad and the shopping spree that followed.

"And this Brad guy is who?"

I told him.

"And he looks like what?"

I told him.

"Ponytail, Guccis without socks, gold chains, and Armani suits? How kitsch. Is he serious or into self-parody?" Christian asked.

"What's kitsch?"

"So tasteless it works," he explained. "Kind of like my new banana dinner jacket. And, Cher, let me get this straight: This Brad dude did a makeover on *you?*"

It did seem funny now. I rubbed my aching calves and gently patted the Band-Aids on my blistered ankles. It felt so fine to be chilling in barefoot sweats and playing catch-up with Christian.

"What's happening in the Windy City?" I asked. And for a prime, mood-altering hour he unloaded on me. Then we sent each other endless kisses and promised to speak again soon.

A minute after I hung up, gloom descended. I felt lonelier than I had before. And extravagantly confused.

Was Christian right regarding my past? I wondered. When I'd taught Tai how to dress like a Beverly Hills hottie on a below Sunset budget, when I'd helped my French cousin Dani dump her two-timing boyfriend and see the light in the worshipful eyes of her homie Jean-Michel, when I'd collected countless cartons of gourmet foods and resort wear for the Pismo Beach flood victims: Was that robbing people of initiative and self-sufficiency? Or was it generously sharing my special gifts with them? Was I just sticking my rhinoplasty-free nose into other people's business or, as Christian had said, did I really have a unique and precious talent worth nurturing?

I wished I could ask Daddy. But he was too frenzied. He'd been soaring on a sugar-and-caffeine buzz for days, completely buried in legal briefs and crusty takeout containers. He didn't have time for me now.

I stared at the stack of books in front of me. I couldn't read anymore. I was in leadership overload. I couldn't listen to tapes. My head was clogged with self-affirming meditations. I couldn't think of a single person I could comfortably reach out and touch by cellular tonight. And I'd already done my StairMaster and step routines.

A pigout beckoned. Or maybe a TV binge. One of those mindless remote-flipping, station-hopping, couch potato trips.

I'd hit bottom. It was like being sucked into the vortex of ickiness. Is this all there is? I wondered.

Chapter 14

I peeled myself off the sofa and wandered out of the den. There was a light on in Daddy's office. I found myself moving toward it. It was golden and warm and spilled out across the marble hallway onto the portrait of my mother.

"Hey, what's happenin', Ma?" I asked, looking up at her gentle smile and way poufed seventies hair. "So what do you think about the all-new improved me? Cool, huh? No more rescuing the clueless. I've totally retired from that gig. Today it's about me. About self-esteem, self-sufficiency, self-awareness. I'm focusing strictly on myself."

She didn't seem all that impressed.

"Cher, get in here," Daddy bellowed.

"Whoops, gotta split, Ma. Catch you later," I said.

Daddy was pacing in front of his desk. His tie,

which totally didn't work with his vest, was unknotted. His shirt collar was unbuttoned. He was swigging black coffee from a paper cup.

"I need some help here," he said. "Everything's gotten all jumbled up. I want you to go over that stack of depositions and put them in order by date. Can you do that for me?"

There was nothing I'd rather have done. "Of course," I said, grinning at him.

"I like the way you look tonight," Daddy said stiffly.

"Excuse me?"

"I mean, better than that weird way you've been dressing lately. Here." He gathered up a pile of blue-bound legal papers that had been scattered over his desk and handed them to me. "What's going on with you, anyway?" he demanded.

"What do you mean, Daddy?"

"Those new clothes you bought—they're too grown up. And those stupid shoes. You're lucky you just got blisters, not a nosebleed from them. They are too high for someone your age. And where are Dionne and that other jerk you hang out with? The clumsy one from Brooklyn? Usually I can't sit down to a meal without one of them having a crisis and storming in here or at least telephoning."

I was stunned. I couldn't believe Daddy had caught all that. I'd thought he was too busy, too single-mindedly focused on work, to notice or care about me that way.

"I don't know how to tell you this, Cher," he said, running his fingers through his hair. He hadn't stopped pacing. He wasn't actually looking at me either. "But there are going to be some changes around here. Big changes."

My heart lurched. I blurted out the first thing that came into my mind. "Does this have anything to do with Harriet?"

"Plenty."

"Are you getting married, Daddy?"

"To whom?"

"Harriet Goddard."

He stopped pacing and frowned angrily at me. "What's the matter with you, Cher? What're you talking about, me marrying Harriet?"

"Well, she's attractive, bright, self-sufficient. . . . You respect her, right?"

"Of course I respect her. I respect my partner, Sy Rapaport, too, but I wouldn't marry him—even if he didn't eat like a pig. What in the world made you think I would marry Harriet?"

"Well, you said this had something to do with her."

"It has. Don't get me wrong, I like Harriet. She's a smart, good-looking woman. Her connections are terrific. She's introduced me to more prospective clients in the past couple of weeks than I've met in years. And of course I was very flattered by how much she wanted me to work with her. I like the way she came after me. But that's all business."

Business? I was awash in confusion. I mean, I'd seen Harriet practically picking out Daddy's wardrobe. And what about all that beaming?

"What I don't like," Daddy continued, "is the way

she seems to be influencing you. That's what I mean. Those shoes, that lips-of-death makeup you've started wearing, those big-shouldered suits. Enough already! That's what's going to change, young lady. And when was the last time you told me to take my vitamins?"

"But, Daddy, I thought you hate when I do that."

"What do you care if I hate it? It's a dirty job, Cher, but someone's got to do it." He gulped the last of his cold coffee, crumpled the cup, and hurled it into the wastebasket behind his desk. "You want me to die of takeout ptomaine?"

"Not even! I want you to live forever, Daddy." I jumped up and kissed him.

He grinned at me. "All right, all right. Enough. We've got work to do."

We sat down opposite each other, and he began to sort through the mess on his desk.

"I don't know if I'll ever forgive you for sending Josh away," Daddy grumbled. "He's got such a good head on his shoulders, and he's such a decent, helpful kid. What do you hear from him? When is he coming back?"

While I flipped through the pile of depos Daddy had given me, I explained what had happened during my last phone call with Josh. "So I haven't heard from him since he hung up on me. Which, of course, I totally deserved."

The telephone rang. Daddy looked around for his cellular.

"Your console is lit," I told him. He nodded, turned to his desk phone, and hit the speaker button.

"Mel, hi. It's Harriet Goddard."

"Hey, Harriet. We were just talking about you. Cher's here, helping me out with some legal work."

"You're a lucky guy, Mel. That's one self-possessed kid you're rearing. I've rarely met a young woman as poised, proactive, and principle-centered."

Daddy winked at me.

"Thanks, Harriet," I called. "We're on speakerphone."

"Cher? Hello! I called Mel because I've got two tickets to a benefit tomorrow night. Big American Film Institute do. And, Mel, while you know how much I admire your work ethic and your single-minded perseverance, it's my purpose to persuade you to join me. Is that an option?"

Daddy shrugged and looked searchingly at me.

You need a night off, I mouthed. "Totally viable," I told Harriet.

She laughed her rich, creamy laugh. "Is that a yes, Mel?"

I nodded at Daddy like crazy. Finally he said, "Doable," and winked at me.

"Harriet, I've been meaning to ask you," I interrupted. "What does *bankable* mean—as in Brad Dietz?"

"That his reputation is strong enough to count on, to bank on. Which reminds me . . . Cher, are you still there?"

"Proactively present," I called.

"Perfect. I don't quite know how to say this . . ." Now, here was something new. Harriet Goddard without a clue? She actually sounded hesitant. "I spoke with Brad a few minutes ago. He's . . . how can I put it? In a negative space, I guess. In stress mode. His principles and values are . . . Well, Brad's experiencing the need to shift, or even rescript, his basic paradigm."

"You mean he's in a monster funk? . . . Like having a Prozac moment?"

"Exactly."

"Want me to speed-dial him?"

"Would you?"

"Bank on it." I glanced over at Daddy. He nodded, go. I threw him a kiss and headed for my room, pausing in the hallway for a quality moment with Mom.

"Self-assured, self-esteem, self-aware, self-sufficient. I should've known you wouldn't go for all that hyphenated self stuff," I told her. "It's so Me Decade, so 1980s, right? Anyway, you're the one I take after, Ma. You're my do-good paradigm."

Who says transformation takes time? I phoned Brad and changed my life in three minutes flat. Harriet was right. Brad was buggin'. He was practically postal with despair. This was a big day for firsts. First Harriet Goddard had been at a loss for words. Now Brad was in a crisis of confidence. Brad and arrogance, yes. Brad and self-doubt? A formerly reliable, Not even!

He picked up the phone after six rings and sounded like, zombie world, hello!

"Wow, you must be hurting big time," I blurted. "Where's that slammin' egomaniac élan? Where's that bouncy Brad-knows-best sound? Talk to me, director man."

He did. For minute one, he tried a totally faux light

'n' breezy thing. He went, "Cher! Hey, how you doing? Good to hear from you." It was all yadda-yadda-yadda upbeat show-biz sham.

I just listened in empowering, supportive silence until he ran out of steam. Then the truth broke free. Brad had taken an unscheduled cruise on the Love Boat without a flotation device. He was brutally sprung on a college coed who did not return the compliment.

"I'm in love," he confessed, his deep, assertive voice warbling with misery. "I've found the perfect woman, Cher. She's bright, sensitive, a grad-school film student who loves my movies—both of them. She's seen my AFI project about a dozen times. Ditto the twenty-minute documentary I did for Harriet. The one that earned a prize at Telluride two years ago. She's crazy about my work but not about me."

"Initials are?" I asked.

"You know her," Brad said.

And I did. "L.R., right? It's Lauren."

"Lauren Roberts." The warble gave way to a sigh. "Cher, did you ever wake up and realize, in one split second, that someone you'd seen and talked to and taken for granted forever was suddenly the most important person in your life? The one you relied on without even knowing it? The one whose smile could get you through a rough day, whose honesty and integrity was not just refreshing to you but essential?"

Of course I'm thinking about Josh and nodding my golden head and silently going, yes, yes, yes, when suddenly Brad says, "No. You're too young, Cher. You wouldn't understand."

"As if!" I huffed. "Nice to know your arrogance isn't totally mashed."

"She hates that, too. My arrogance . . . the way I dress . . . the limousine and attitude thing I get into . . . And I'm clueless, Cher. I'm absolutely lost here. I need help."

"You need what?" I asked.

"Help, Cher," Brad repeated. "I need help."

There they were. The magic words I'd been waiting for. The three little words that released me from my enchanted state. I blinked and a haze seemed to lift from my eyes, like when a monster pressure inversion clears the smog off Malibu. My room, which had become a lonely wasteland, seemed suddenly bright with possibilities again, and very tastefully decorated.

"Brad, this is so doable," I said with real enthusiasm.

For three weeks I had worked on transforming myself from a do-gooder to a go-getter. I had weathered a way exhausting info blitz, severe peer pressure, the disintegration of valued relationships, and blisters like you would not believe.

Now, after three brutal weeks, it had taken only three minutes and those three little words—*I need help*—to change my mind and turn me into a true power player. I was no longer Harriet's clone. I was not Brad's Barbie doll. Someone needed me, and suddenly I was all principle-centered, competent, committed. I had achieved personal perfection.

I was so ready to move on.

Chapter 15

Socks," I said to Murray. "Bring a bag full of those new Calvins you've been wearing, in like celery, ecru, and beige shades. The man does not own a single pair." I checked "Socks" off the list on my clipboard.

Tai squeezed in beside me on the bench. "I couldn't find Travis," she reported breathlessly, "but I know he'll show up, Cher. Only skateboarding isn't as easy as it looks. Your friend might get destroyed."

"Brad is in serious need of a loosening-up experience, Tai. And who better than Travis to tutor him? But you're right. We'll load him up with safety features—helmet, elbow and knee pads, air bags, whatever. Can you take that on?"

"Oh, sure," Tai said. "I've got a lot of that gear at home. And you want me to bring over my comic books, too?"

"Let's call them graphic novels." I took a sip of the caffeine-free diet soda Janet had set down in front of me, then studied my list again.

We were hanging at our reserved table in the Quad. The whole Crew was there. The calls I'd made after speaking to Brad last night had been short and to the point. I need your help, I had confided to one friend after another. It was way heartwarming. Not one of them had refused me.

Well, Dionne had held out for a while. "Come on, girlfriend," I'd begged her. "This is going to be the makeover of the year, maybe the century—and there's even a little matchmaking thrown in. De, I can't do it without you."

"I thought you were so over that stuff."

"I changed my mind. It's important not to be inflexible. Anyway, it's different if someone asks for help," I explained. "And I'm not doing a major ego trip or anything. I mean, this will be a group effort."

"What're you wearing to school tomorrow?" she'd asked cautiously.

"Skinny rib sweater, micro skirt, thigh-highs, cute hat."

"Shoes?"

"Midcalf lace-up boots, chunky heels. You hated my exec look, right?"

"I don't want to be all judgmental, but, yes. It totally blew."

"That's what Daddy said, too," I'd confessed, "but not as eloquently. See you tomorrow, girlfriend?"

"For sure. I'll swing by in the A.M. and pick you up."

"You want me to cut his hair?" Dionne asked now. "I kind of like it. I mean, it reminds me of . . ."

"I know. Me, too." I looked up from my clipboard and grinned at her. "Antonio Banderas, right?"

"Actually," De said, "I was thinking more like Karl Lagerfeld. He's this excellent clothing and fragrance designer," she explained to Ringo Farbstein, whose head had done a little tilt thing at the mention of the ponytailed couturier. "We hit his place in Paris."

"That's just the point, De," I clarified. "Lagerfeld is like a million years old, plus he's always fanning himself like he's totally plagued by exhaustion. Brad needs a new look. A young look. I mean, he's midtwenties, max. He's got a few good years left."

"Okay, the ponytail. Survey says?" De looked around the table. Murray, Elton, Baez, and, of course, the hair-impaired empress herself, Amber, each gave a thumbs down.

"Ponytail goes," De conceded.

"Phat," I said, then I turned to Ringo and Janet. "Sorry, you kids." I turned the clipboard around and showed them where I'd crossed their names off the list. "I checked with him. Turns out he's excellent at math. But please come anyway. It would be frantically empowering to have your support."

"Is he agile?" Janet asked.

"I really don't know," I said.

"He's not even old," Tai offered.

"Agile, not fragile," Ringo explained to Tai. "*Agile* means able to bend and move well. Like dancers and gymnasts. Janet used to be a gymnast and she's a righteous dancer."

"Brainstorm. Perfect, perfect," I said, tapping my

pencil eraser against my chin. "Okay, Janet, you can teach him a few moves. Murray, as discussed, you're on for clothes in general, socks in particular. And he needs a major CD overhaul. Elton, that's your number one priority. I want him musically revised and updated, ASAP, which means "as soon as possible." Think of yourself as an organ donor, Elton. Brad needs like a total MTV transplant. So that's it. My house, immediately after school today."

"Excuse me? Today, as in *Friday?* As in beginning of the *weekend?*" Amber whined. "And you are going to do *what,* Cher? I mean, you are so busy assigning everyone else—"

"Cher's coordinating and supervising the makeover," De explained, "because she's got the most management training."

"Well, there's a stunning surprise." Amber faked a giant yawn. "Like I could not have guessed that? I am *so* speechless. Well, Ms. Management, what is my job?"

I gave her a nurturing smile. This wasn't my makeover, it was ours. If I'd learned anything in the past couple of weeks, it was that the support of my friends was important. That we could do together what I couldn't do alone. This was my first cooperative makeover. I was living a paradigm of interdependence.

"Do something you're really good at, Amber," I suggested.

"Yeah," De said, "like dress badly and complain."

Actually, there were a couple of items left on my list that needed speedy doing. Before the makeover began, I had to snag a videotape of *Moviemaker,* Brad's award-winning documentary. Then I had to get Lauren to come by tomorrow night and watch it with me. Last, but definitely not least, I needed to call Josh to try to repair our long-distance misunderstanding. I was totally prepared to grovel.

The first two items turned out to be a snap. Lauren answered the phone at Goddard Productions. I told her I was trying to find a video print of Brad's second movie. She said there was one in the office and if I really needed it, she could drop it off on her way home from work.

"What are you doing tonight?" I asked her.

"Same as always. Studying. I've got a paper due."

"How about you work on the paper first, then come by and watch Brad's movie with me? I mean, I don't really know anything deep about films except a few new words. But I'm vitally interested. We could, you know, talk about editing and turnaround options and sitcom syndie deals. Send out to Spago for a pizza."

"I don't think Spago delivers, Cher. So you've never seen *Moviemaker* before? It's a brilliant little film. Actually, it's all about Brad. The *real* Brad." Lauren laughed. "It shows him as a kid shooting home movies. He's already directing. He's seeing images, positioning his grandfather against the light, experimenting with angles and these extraordinary zoom shots. You can see his seriousness, his intensity. And he's only about eight or nine years old. That passion of his, it gives you goosebumps."

Tscha!

Was Brad mental? He thought this hottie wasn't

sparked by him? As if! No subtitles required to get this picture. Maybe Lauren wasn't picking out kitchen curtains yet, but she was definitely pro-Dietz.

"You like him, right?"

She laughed again. "I think he's a proper director, if that's what you mean. I wouldn't mind seeing the flick again. Tell you what, I'll bring the pizza. What time is good for you?"

"Excellent," I enthused. I thought about what lay ahead. Only the most brutal makeover Beverly Hills High's A-list had ever attempted. We had our work cut out for us. "Is nine P.M. too late?" My fingers were crossed. Between loosening-up lessons and a major music infusion, earlier than that was risky.

"Gives me time to get a little writing done. Nine's fine," Lauren said.

Yes!

Two down and one to go. I stashed my cellular and headed home.

My priorities were way clear. Before Brad and the makeover crew arrived, I would phone Josh. Apply damage control to our relationship. Apologize for my ego-driven insensitivity. And accept his assurances that I was still number one in his mind and heart.

Do not ask me why but, somewhere between starting my Jeep in the school parking lot and screeching to a halt on the cobblestone driveway in front of our house, I began to wonder whether it would be that easy. Was it possible that Josh might not forgive me?

Self-doubt is not something I do well. If you spell-

112

checked my brain, you wouldn't even find *insecure* listed. But the whack seed had been planted. Like, what if Josh was really mad at me?

Suddenly rejection, another word I rarely have reason to use, seemed possible.

I popped my seat belt and hurried into the house. Daddy was gone, as expected. He was meeting Harriet in town for the big AFI event. I dropped my backpack, hit the kitchen, and threw open the freezer door.

There was a gallon drum of chocolate swirl frozen yogurt on the middle shelf. I tore open the lid. The container was empty. Not a decent lick left. "LUCY!" I hollered. There was no answer. Then I heard her orthopedic shoes scuttling toward the utility closet. "It's okay. Never mind, Luce," I shouted. "Sorry."

I shut the freezer door, hurried across the room, and lifted the crystal top off our Steuben cookie jar.

My emergency Oreos were gone.

It took massive strength of character not to wet my finger and troll for crumbs along the bottom of the jar. But I had my pride. I replaced the heavy cut-glass lid.

The kitchen clock warned me that Brad was due in ten minutes, De in five. The rest of the Crew would soon follow. I was running out of time. Stressed or not, I had to call Josh now.

I took a deep breath, then exhaled. Just do it, my Nike voice said. Only this time, it could have been Mom's voice. Or maybe Michael Jordan's or one of those really tall athletic people who make gazillions in sportswear endorsements.

Just do it.

I perched on a kitchen stool next to the wall phone and dialed the Seattle number.

After a couple of rings, Josh's mom picked up. "Cher. Oh, I'm so glad it's you," she said. "I was going to phone you myself this afternoon. I didn't think you'd be home just yet."

"Wow, you sound golden, Gail. Way superior to last time." It was true. Josh's bright and bubbly mom no longer sounded like a victim of extraterrestrial experiments. The alien abduction thing was over.

"Thanks," she said. "I owe so much of it to you, Cher. Josh told me."

"Told you what?"

"That his coming up here was your idea. That you insisted on it. I'm so grateful. I couldn't have asked him myself. But I really don't know what I would have done without him. I was feeling so rotten, Cher. And he's been such an angel. So thanks. And how are you, honey?"

"Oh, I'm okay. So you and Harold are . . ."

"Didn't Josh tell you? Harold's back home. He came back a couple of days ago, just as Josh predicted. Of course, I didn't believe him. But you know Josh, how smart and sensible he is. It was his idea that we go up to the cabin for a few days. I was a terrible mess," Gail continued. "I'd worried myself into nervous exhaustion. I couldn't sleep, couldn't eat. The cabin was perfect. The mountain air cleared my head and, unfortunately . . ." Gail giggled. "It gave me back my appetite. And when Josh and I got back to the city, well, Harold had left a dozen frantic messages. He's really so sweet."

"That's chronic, Gail. I'm way happy for you." I glanced at the clock. "Gail, is Josh around?"

"Around? Well, I . . . Here, you mean?"

Uh-oh, had alien invaders returned to claim Gail? "Yes. Is Josh there with you . . . or is he at the library or something?"

"Cher, Josh is in Los Angeles. Don't tell me you didn't know. He flew back yesterday morning."

Oreos! my brain screamed.

Josh was back in town, and he hadn't even called me. "Got to go, Gail," I said, adding a little upbeat chuckle to hide my crushing disappointment. "I'm like so glad that everything worked out for you and Harold. It's the bomb, really. Way excellent."

Oreos wouldn't even have done the trick, I realized after I'd hung up. What I really craved was some million-calorie, nutritionally empty, plastic food product primarily composed of refined sugar.

Chapter 16

*T*here wasn't even time to tell De what I'd just learned. She rushed breathlessly into my house juggling multiple shopping bags.

"Dionne, you're only responsible for cutting Brad's hair. How many pairs of scissors do you need?"

"Excuse me, is there a control problem here? This is *my* contribution to your friend's new look." She brushed past me into our domed entry hall.

"Not even!" I protested. "It was just a fact-gathering moment."

De gave me a big, beautiful smile and began downloading the contents of her bags onto the marble top of our million-year-old Louis-the-something table. I had never seen her so psyched about a makeover.

"Mousse, extra-hold gel, scissors, styling spray, volumizer, shampoos for fine, normal, and full-bodied hair. You didn't specify hair type, did you?" she asked. "Conditioners, of course. Protein rinse—" She stopped abruptly and began sweeping everything back into its appointed bag. "Anyway, girlfriend, you ought to thank me for all the thought I've put into this. I only wish you'd told me we were going to be stars."

"Excuse me?"

"This is so down," she said, practically squealing. "They're right outside!"

"And by 'they' you mean?" I asked.

De dragged me to the front door and opened it with a flourish.

Travis was standing there, skateboard under his arm. His hand was poised above the door chimes. He clutched his heart and stepped back. "Wow, your bell is like way sensitive. Beyond cybertech. I didn't even know I rang it yet."

De rolled her eyes. "Excuse us, Travis." She moved him to one side.

"Cool." He grinned at me. "Cher, dude, I've never like been in a movie."

There was an industrial-strength van blocking our parking court. It had an old-fashioned movie camera stenciled on its side above the words "Set Jetters— The Movie People." From the van, a crew I'd never seen before was dragging electrical cables, wheeling wooden crates, and carrying metal boxes toward the house. Brad Dietz was overseeing the operation. Tai and Amber were looking on, slack-jawed with awe.

"Cher!" Brad crunched across the cobblestones, bare-ankled in his Guccis, and kissed the air beside my cheekbones. "I hope you don't mind. I just smelled something exciting here, something bold."

Travis took a step back and tried to look casual as he sniffed the armpits of his Bob Marley signature T-shirt.

"It smelled," Brad clarified excitedly, "like a movie. I've got to do this, Cher. I've got to shoot this transformation. It's a big transitional moment for me. Look," he said.

He unfolded a sheaf of long papers on which someone had drawn what looked like a comic strip without the speech balloons. The cartoon boxes were numbered. "I stayed up most of last night thinking this through. I even got a friend to storyboard it for me. That's what this is." Brad hit the comic strip pages. "See, it's a scene-by-scene diagram of the action."

A horn sounded behind the van. De's cellular went off. She took the call and said, "Oh, hi, Murray. Where are you?"

"He's out here," Tai reported from the street. "He can't get into the driveway. And Elton's Porsche is right behind him."

"Guys," Brad called to his helpers, although two of them were girls. "We've got to move the truck. Let these kids in. Just give us a couple of minutes to set up, okay?" Brad asked me. "Moira, Tony, let's go inside and take a light reading."

Moira and Tony were Brad's camera people. Ike was his AD—assistant director, Brad explained. He introduced them to me, then hurried into the house.

Following quickly behind them, a guy in a baseball

cap, shlepping a tripod and lights, bumped into me. I spun around, bouncing off a brawny blond whose workshirt said his name was Tom. He had a thick coil of cable wire over one shoulder and was carrying a couple of silver umbrellas. "What is this place?" he asked, catching my arm and steadying me.

"It's only my home," I replied, brushing cable crud off my red spandex tube dress. "And it is so not fully insured. Plus my father, a totally prominent attorney, gets furiously irate if anything is even out of place. Not to mention broken—"

"We'll be very careful," Tom promised.

"Come on." De grabbed my hand. "Let's go find Brad and get started."

"Woman," Murray bellowed, startling us both. Loaded down with suit boxes and dry-cleaning bags, he came hip-hopping around the corner of the van. His face was practically hidden behind the pile of clothes in his arms. Trying to balance the load, Murray tugged up his designer baggies. "You know, I could use a hand here," he growled, peering over the pile at us.

"You got it, dude!" Travis dropped his skateboard and began to applaud.

Murray glared at him. "That's not the kind of hand I meant."

"I'm sorry, Murray," I said, "but De and I have a schedule to adhere to. Travis, Ringo, can you help Murray carry the clothing, please?"

"It's okay," Tai said. "Amber and I'll do it. Travis has to meditate."

"Medicate?" Murray asked.

"Medi*tate*," Tai corrected him.

"It's like a spiritual balance thing, you know?" Travis shrugged modestly. "I mean, everyone thinks like skateboarding is all fanatical control. No way. It's about being laid back and loose. If I'm going to show this Brad dude how to do it, I've got to get like centered, make contact with the Big Boardmeister."

"Whatever." Amber made the W sign.

"Um-believable." Tai stared up at Travis, starry-eyed. "Come on, Amber, Murray is like desperate for our help."

"Carry dry-cleaning bags? Love to," Amber said sarcastically. "There is *so* no business like show business, is there?"

Brad's word was golden. He and his crew had converted my quarters to a movie set in like no time. De and I followed the cable wires snaking up the plushly carpeted stairway, across the gold-leafed balcony, down the paneled hallway, and into my pastel-accented room.

Silver reflector umbrellas amplified the wincingly bright lights that Tom and the techies had set up. Moira was checking out everything through her camera lens. She was all, "Is that an Aubusson carpet? You have clothes racks that actually rotate? You sleep in a king-size hand-carved four-poster?"

De and I were all like, doesn't everyone?

Brad went into a huddle with Moira. They decided to have her assistant, Tony, shoot a video version of the goings-on. "I want some footage with a home-movie feel," Brad explained. "Video is immediate, informal. It's got a kind of amateurish integrity."

Amber and Tai followed Murray into the room. "Where does this stuff go, Cher?" Tai asked.

"Let's see." I checked my clipboard. "We'll unpack the ensembles and color-code them over there." I pointed with my pencil. "Set them out on the bed. Dark to light. Socks and shoes to match. Excellent."

Brad broke away from Tom and the baseball hat guy. "You must be Murray. You're doing wardrobe, right?"

Murray shook Brad's extended hand, then stepped back to study him.

"I'm Tai," Tai said, grinning at Brad. He offered her his hand. She leaned forward to take it and tripped over a taped-down cable line.

Brad helped her up. "And you are?" He turned to Amber.

"Just a bit player eager to do my part." She fluttered her eyelash extenders at him.

"I can't look." De shut her eyes. "Is he hurling?"

"Well, what's the verdict?" Brad asked Murray.

"Too much gold and much too old. You know what I'm saying? Cher was on the money. You've got accessory problems, bro. And that big-shouldered look?" Murray shook his head sadly. "Don't be fooled. It is not your friend. It's your basic last year at the All-Star Café thing. Total tourist."

"I hope you've got enough juice to handle all this," Elton announced from the doorway. He pulled down his sunglasses and surveyed the room. "I'm not risking choice disks on a power failure waiting to happen. I haven't seen such a setup for disaster since Courtney Love blew the amps at the Hole concert and jammed the electric parking-lot gates."

Big blond Tom laughed. "The lights are hooked up to a power generator in the van. That's what these cables are all about."

"I knew that," Elton said. "Cher, where's your sound system?"

"Bookshelves." I waved my pencil in their direction. "Behind the leatherbound complete works of Charles Dickens. They're faux," I explained.

Elton nodded and carried his CD case over to the bookshelves.

"Faux Dickens?" Moira was having a hard time with the concept.

"They're not real books," I explained. "It's just this pull-out panel I had specially designed to hide my new entertainment center. It just looks like books. But if you're like hungry for cultural enrichment, Daddy has a total set of decent Dickens in the den."

"Okay, kids." Brad clapped his hands. "Let's do this thing. Moira, the storyboard is just a rough outline. Follow it loosely. Add anything that amuses you. Get playful, creative. Take it all in. We've got"—he looked at his watch—"less than two hours. Okay, Cher, where do you want to start?"

"Let's save the worst for first," I said. "Say goodbye to Mr. Ponytail."

"You don't expect me to play my CDs on this system, do you?" Elton called from the bookcase.

"Elton, it's brutally next generation. Daddy just bought it."

"Today?" Elton asked suspiciously.

"Duh, like of course," I fibbed.

"Yeah, what time?"

"Oh, use your own system then." It was way humiliating not being state of the art in front of everyone.

"Okay. I'll be right back," Elton said. "My portable CD player's in the Porsche."

Brad sat down at my dressing table and grinned into the three-way mirror. De unpacked two pairs of scissors and her pink-capped atomizer can of Evian mineral water. "Are you ready?" she asked, pointing the spray at Brad's thick dark hair.

"I am. Moira, Tony, you ready? Ike? Okay, let's go."

"Quiet on the set!" Ike bellowed. "Okay, three, two, one . . . And we are *rolling!*"

Brad Dietz came out beyond my wildest expectations. De did a totally excellent styling. She gave Brad a nice but not excessively neat look. A kind of ragged, kind of rugged, kind of thing. I especially liked that she'd left plenty of hair for Lauren to run her fingers through.

For a self-confessed opinionated and arrogant guy, Brad was like stunningly open to change. He kept going, "You think this works? I think it'll work. How's it look, Moira? You think she'll go for it? I think she'll go for it. Did you get it on tape, Tony?" All he cared about was Lauren, and the movie, of course.

Elton's selections provided a seriously stomping soundtrack not only for the haircut and shave but for Murray's piece of the makeover. Although De did a forceful thumbs down on the hip-hop look.

"Don't even think about it," she warned, shaking a finger in Murray's face. "Those old draggy baggies and backward caps are severely vintage. They're a total cliché. Get over it, Murray. The man needs attitude, not platitude."

"I'm not committed to urban here. I never intended on doing a 'hood thing with the brother," Murray protested. "I see my mission as weaning the man from the Gucci-Armani nexus. Going U.S.A. all the way. You know, J. Crew and Gap natural, Timberlands on his feet with L.L. Bean or Calvin crew socks inside them."

"Josh-wear," De said, approvingly. Then she looked over at me. "When's your man coming home, anyway?"

"He's home. Details to follow," I said, cutting my eyes at Amber, who was suddenly alert and listening with rampant interest.

While Travis and Tai took Brad around the block for an attitude adjustment, the Set Jetters crew packed up their equipment. "How'd he do?" I asked Moira, when she returned from filming Brad's skateboard session.

She was decently impressed. "I don't think the board will ever become Brad's primary means of transportation, but he did display a certain aptitude and surprising grace."

"He didn't fall?"

"Not once. Your friend Travis is a terrific teacher. A laid-back guru of the art. He was very eloquent, actually, explaining how you don't master the board so much as become one with it. And his friend—Tai, right?—she's a perfect foil for Travis. Where he's cool, she's hot. Where he's slow, she's fast. They're a great couple, aren't they? Kind of like a squirrel and a tree."

"Made for each other," Amber chimed in, glancing longingly at Elton.

We took a Perrier break, then Moira, Tony, and Ike headed down to the flagstone patio around the pool where Janet and Elton were enhancing Brad's rhythm skills. De, Tai, and I watched from the terrace as Janet demonstrated simple yet effective dance moves while Elton DJed the event.

"Okay, here's the difference between Nirvana and Foo Fighters," Elton shouted over the sounds of his portable CD player. "Can you hear that? The Foo is like Nirvana minus all that tacky pain. But it's a full cut above intellectual bubble gum music. . . . Whereas Dish, the coed combo, has a heavy punk line with a Hollywood Bowl concert edge. But if you're like an Elastica head, you could check out Rusted Root for killer buzz."

From the terrace, you could see the improvement in Brad's energy level and hip-pumping skill. Even Janet Hong stopped, finally, and applauded her pupil. Elton shut off the music and gave Brad a high five. Then the laughing trio, with Travis, who'd been sunning on a nearby chaise longue, and Moira and Ike made their way back to the house.

My makeover team was exhausted but triumphant. I thought a perky yet brutally sincere thank-you was in order. "This way, people," I beckoned. "Please follow me to the entrance hall."

Our vestibule is circular and seriously impressive. It soars three stories to a skylit dome. Beneath that dome, from our wrought-iron and gilt-trimmed balcony, twin staircases, each one cushioned in deep pile carpeting, wind down to a polished pink marble floor.

"Wait here, please," I urged, hurrying up the stairs as quickly as my tube dress permitted. They were all there—Brad, Moira, Tony, Tom, Ike, and my people—staring up at me expectantly.

I clutched the wrought-iron railing. "So, people, listen up," I called to them. "I've got to have some time alone with Brad before Lauren gets here. But I want to personally thank each and every one of you."

Amber did her eye-rolling I-am-so-bored thing.

"Yes, *everyone*," I emphasized, "especially those of you who have overcome your own fierce personal challenges—like impaired taste and bad hair—to show up for and seriously support Brad today. Together we have achieved a fully righteous transformation. We have helped a significant and bankable young talent move from a self-directed to a principle-centered way of life. A way of life that is more about quality than quantity, American values not European clothing. And need I address the gold accessories issue? I think not."

Dionne began to applaud. Murray, Ringo, and Janet Hong joined her. Ike and Brad were laughing and slapping high fives. Tai and Travis went wild, whistling and cheering. Moira was laughing delightedly and, of course, filming the entire event. Amber, I was stunned to notice, was tearfully blotting her over-made-up eyes.

Suddenly Elton hit the Play button on his portable CD box. Music exploded. It was this completely archaic yet flaming version of "The Star Spangled Banner."

"Jimi Hendrix, my man!" Murray identified the disk.

"Um-believable!" Tai shrieked, jumping up and down, hanging on to Travis's arm. "It's a total time warp. It's like, arise Woodstock nation!"

Brad said something to Travis, who nodded vigorously, then rushed out of the entry hall, returning a minute later with two skateboards. Travis handed one to Brad, and they ran up the twin staircases to my balcony.

The Hendrix anthem continued.

Brad winked at me. Then he and Travis skateboarded down the stairs. Brad went down one side, Travis down the other. They hit bottom as the song ended. Travis topped off his performance with a series of way impressive wheelies. Brad jumped off his board and began to boogie with Janet to the next selection, which was from Elton's favorite Sponge album, "Rotting Piñata."

I thought the music blew, but looking down at my partying homies, my heart swelled with pride and love. Together, we had gone where no makeover team had dared to go before. We had pulled off a brutal two-hour top-to-toe way-deep transformation. If the Book of World Records had a makeover section, our names would be totally inscribed.

Chapter 17

*T*he house was quiet. The Set Jetters had done an excellent job in the tidying-up division. Lucy and I had cleared away the snacks and Perrier debris. Now it was just Brad and me—with Moira shooting the scene, this time with a videocam—engaged in the last chore on my list. Clipboard said, "Assignment: What a t.b. Betty really wants." And under the column headed "Support Team" I'd written "Cher." This one was mine.

"Now, notice the way Josh walks in this shot," I was telling Brad. "It's confident yet humble. It says, 'I know who I am, and I'd like to get to know you.' Can you see that? The way he's moving toward that guy. Like he's shy, but he'll get over it to make you feel comfortable."

Brad and I were watching videotapes in the den. We were sitting side by side on the sofa, our fingertips turning orange from cheese-puffs dust. Brad was holding the crinkly bag of Chee•tos. I was playing couch commando with the VCR remote. Moira, peering through her camera at us, was across the room in Daddy's old Eames chair.

Brad's Timberlands were resting on the coffee table. Sitting there, staring at the television screen, he looked eerily like Josh. The accessible yet appealing generic mall clothing. The clean-shaven boyish good looks. The whole bright-eyed Baldwin aura.

"Is that you?" Brad asked me, pointing at the TV. "In that little pink dress?"

"Pay attention to Josh," I said. "He's the basic good guy paradigm we're after. Notice that even in formal wear, there's that clean Eddie Bauer breath of fresh air about him."

I hadn't realized how difficult this part of Brad's makeover was going to be. This was not *Buns of Steel* we were watching, or some glossy, impersonal tape of Cindy Crawford doing the Reebok bounce. These were videos of Josh, my first and only love—not counting close relatives, of course. They were up close and personal tapes, taken at meaningful moments in our relationship.

There was my PC man, dressed to thrill, at the Hall-Geist nuptials. And there I was, it was true, a total vision in bridesmaid pink.

"Wait, wait. Look at that." I tugged Brad's sleeve. "You see the way he's looking at me there?" I hit the pause button on the remote. "That's the look, that's the feeling you want to communicate to Lauren. What does that say to you?"

"Well, it's evident," Brad responded. "It says 'love,' right? I mean, the guy is clearly crazy about you."

I reached forward and grabbed a couple of Calvin Klein paper napkins off the coffee table. They were very elegant. Dove gray with a quiet burgundy stripe. We used to have Ralph Lauren, but they were cloth and Lucy has enough ironing to do.

I blew my nose into the Calvin. "Do you think so?" I asked. "I mean, I thought so, but—"

"Cher, are you crying?" Brad said.

"Not even!" I protested. "I'm just . . . so moved by your evolutionary transformational growth . . . and by the trust-based teamwork my t.b. posse performed today." I looked back at the image frozen on the TV screen. "So you think he's crazy about me?" I asked Brad, releasing the pause button and setting Josh in motion again. "I mean, I thought so once. I thought he loved me."

"And what changed your mind?"

I blew my nose again. "Well, I hate to admit this, but I messed up. First I sent Josh to Seattle against his better judgment because I thought his mother needed his help—which, it turns out, she definitely did. But Daddy needed Josh, too, and got totally moody. And naturally I also missed Josh. So like everyone was buggin', and it was all my fault. The error of my ways became ruthlessly clear. So I decided to change my entire life."

I was staring morosely at the TV screen, watching Josh play touch football on the beach. His slender bod was barbecued brown. His hair, sandy in the sun, flopped over his forehead as he faded back to receive a pass. He caught the ball that I think Murray had thrown, then turned toward the camera and winked at me. My own eyes misted over again at the sight of his laughing baby blues.

"So then Josh phoned me. And he was practically inert with exhaustion," I continued with a sigh. "I mean he was brutally smoked out from baby-sitting his mom. And I didn't even ask how he was. I just went into this tasteless self-centered rant about my own life—for which I am still riding the shame spiral. Basically, I was unforgivably rude to Josh. So he blew me off. He hung up on me. And now he's back in L.A. and he hasn't even phoned."

Brad motioned to Moira. "Are you getting this whole thing? You going wide with the shot?"

Moira held the camera steady but nodded her head. "Haven't missed a thing, boss. Did you set this up?"

Brad laughed. "I'm a director, not a magician. So tell me, Cher, what would you say to Josh if he were here right now?"

I looked at the TV. Now the video was of Josh at our pool. He was stretched out on a lounge chair reading a hardcover book, probably one that wasn't even assigned. "You see that?" I told Brad. "Reading is another thing you can do to impress Lauren. Just sit around like Josh and be interested in everything. It's very appealing. Plus, I noticed that Lauren is way functional in a bookstore environment."

"You didn't answer the question," Brad said in this weird deep voice that sounded exactly like Josh's. This transformation was going way better than I'd imagined.

I turned to Brad. "So what would you say?" he

asked again. Only Brad Dietz's mouth was not moving. It was all curled in this faux innocent grin.

"Josh?" I said, looking up slowly, with totally palpitating hope, past Brad to the doorway of the den.

He was standing there. In practically the same outfit Brad was wearing. Only Josh was leaner and taller and melt-your-heart fine.

"Well?" he said, crossing his lanky arms in front of him and striking a casual waiting pose. "Was there something you wanted to say to me?"

I leaped up onto the sofa, galloped over Brad's legs, and dove at Josh. Just as I knew he would, he opened his arms and caught me.

After introductions, handshakes, and much laughter at my expense, Moira popped the tape she'd been shooting out of her videocam and gave it to Brad.

"Mind if I check this out?" he asked me.

I was in Josh's arms and not in the mood to mind anything.

"Whatever," I said.

Brad made the W sign. "Whatever," he said to Moira. "Don't you love that?" He ejected the cassette of Josh that we'd been watching and put the makeover tape into the VCR.

While Josh and I got reacquainted, Moira and Brad briefly viewed the video she'd shot. "It's okay," he announced. "Cher, we'd better take off. When's Lauren due?"

"Clipboard says . . . wow, in a fast five! You guys better split."

We walked Brad and Moira to the door, then Josh

and I headed back to the den. "I fibbed," I said. "We've got half an hour."

We snuggled in all cozy, cuddling on our favorite couch, getting happily orange-lipped from exchanging cheese-ball dust, mouth to mouth.

Between kisses I gave Josh the details on Brad, how we'd met, and what was going on. "I wish I had 'before' pictures," I said. "You'd never believe how different he looked. He's really changed."

When I thought about it, I'd really changed, too. For example, admitting my faults is not something I'm overly experienced at. But it was way easy for me to apologize to Josh. He even commented on how nicely I'd done it. Of course, I'd had plenty of practice since he'd been gone. It seemed to me that I'd been apologizing to people for three weeks straight.

"And I'm sorry I hung up on you," he said. "I was so stressed, and then you threw this name at me— Brad. And I . . ."

"Got jealous?"

"As if," Josh teased. "Me, jealous? Like big time, bitterly, full-out jealous? Guilty."

We laughed, and then Josh kept daring me to tell him what I had been going to tell Brad. Which was, of course, that I loved Josh.

"What if he'd asked you why?"

"Why what?" I said. "Why I love you? That is so easy, Josh, that is not even an essay question. Because you have everything I admire and want."

"Flannel shirts and my own apartment?"

"Not even! That is so superficial." I pretended to be annoyed. "You know that I really admire . . . your classic blue eyes," I said, tapping his handsome, high forehead. "Your perfect, orthodontically assisted teeth." I touched his lips. "And that smirky little smile you're giving me right now."

"Oh, and *I'm* superficial?" He laughed.

"Josh." I snuggled closer to him, resting my cheek on his soft washed-denim shirt. "Want to know what I really love and admire about you?" I didn't give him a chance to say no. "Seriously, it's your gentleness. And your convictions and commitment and your emotional strength . . . and especially how your lips taste with cheese-ball dust all over them."

The door chimes sounded. "Whoops." I checked my watch and stood up. "That's Lauren, the Betty that Brad gave up his ponytail for." I pulled Josh to his feet. "Details at eleven. I've got work to do. You're Audi."

He put his arm around me and walked me to the vestibule. "I thought you were finished with match-making and trying to change people."

"Oh, I am," I explained. "But principle-centered etiquette says, if you're invited to help, you really shouldn't refuse. Especially if you've got a highly prized talent to share. Brad did ask for help. And I am so uniquely qualified in this area. Anyway, it was a group project. So I'm not just exercising my ego or actualizing my special gifts, I'm moving from independence to interdependence. Which is grossly evolved."

"Translation?" Josh said.

"In movie terms, subtitle says: Cher is no longer starring in a one-woman show, she's become part of an awesome ensemble."

"Cute."

"Know what's really cute?" I said. "Your lips. Cute and puffy and totally orange." I opened the door as Josh, adorably flustered, licked his lips and tried to rub them clean.

Lauren was standing there with a pizza box in one hand and a videotape cassette tucked under her arm. "Hi," she said. "Is Jethro at home? Never mind." She rolled her eyes and laughed at herself. "Sorry. What a dorky thing to say. I've never delivered pizza to this neighborhood, or to a house this awesome. It's a little intimidating. The Jethro thing was a reference to *The Beverly Hillbillies*. It was supposed to make me feel better. It didn't."

"Intimidated? Daddy would be way joyful," I said, ushering her in. "He totally kvells when people start buggin' over the house. Lauren, this is my boyfriend, Josh. He's just leaving."

"Nice meeting you," Josh said. "Wish I could stay for the picture. I'd love to see Brad's work."

"Really?" I said.

"Hey, stay," said Lauren. "Unless . . ." She looked at me.

I thought it over. The film was twenty minutes long. After that, I'd need privacy for my heart-to-heart with Lauren. "Not a problem," I decided. I took the cassette of *Moviemaker* from her and handed it to Josh. "I'll dish out the pizza. Can you pop this video into the VCR for us, please?"

Lauren and I headed for the kitchen while Josh retired to the den, where, he said, he had some phone calls to make anyway.

The cheese puffs had definitely taken the edge off my hunger. Lauren had picked up a totally decent pie, but all the sight of it stimulated was my gag reflex. She, however, was righteously famished.

"Josh seems really sweet—and seriously smitten," she confided, tearing into the pizza.

"Do you think so?" I got us a couple of Evians.

"Absolutely," Lauren said. "I'm not trying to brag or anything. I mean, that would be a giant chuckle. But I'm usually pretty intuitive about these things."

"You are?" What an opportunity. Total *carpe diem* time. I could not resist. "You mean, you're good at sensing when someone really likes someone else?"

I watched the girl demolish a second slice right from the box. It was refreshing to see a slender Betty who wasn't all that nutritionally correct. In a way I admired her guts. She hadn't even bothered to blot off the excess oil.

"Yes, I am," Lauren said, wiping a trickle of grease from her chin. "But then it wouldn't take a genius to see why someone would fall for you. So, Cher, are you interested in film in general or Brad Dietz's work in particular?"

"Oh, I'm a major moviegoer—mostly of the PG-13 persuasion. Daddy goes ballistic if I even suggest an R. But I do find Brad intriguing. What do you think about him?"

"Ace director. Actually, I'm awed by his talent. I mean he's young and still green, and his work is raw, but in terms of moviemaking, he's the real thing." She smiled and shrugged. "At least as far as I'm concerned."

"Er, that's not exactly what I meant. I mean, I'm in

136

major agreement with you as to Brad's creative and professional abilities. Although, of course, I haven't seen any of his movies yet. But, like, what do you think about him romantically? You know, intuitively. Do you have an intuitive sense about who he likes?"

"Brad Dietz?" I thought I saw a glint of interest in her proper green eyes, but she shut them and mischievously put her hands to her head like a psychic getting a message from beyond.

"Yes, yes," she said, "I've got it." Then she opened her eyes and dropped the charade. "Cher, Brad is crazy about Brad. I'm not knocking his taste, either. He's just totally self-absorbed."

Josh strolled into the kitchen.

"Pizza?" Lauren offered.

Josh thanked her and helped himself to a slice. "What about that movie?"

"Are we ready?" I asked.

"I am," Lauren said, wiping her hands on a napkin and closing the pizza box. "Wait." Her eyes narrowed suspiciously. "Cher, you don't have your own screening room, do you?"

"As if!" I said. "I mean, intimidating is one thing. Ostentatious is furiously another."

Chapter 18

Strategic planning is totally crucial to the success of any project. All the management strategy books I had listened to went postal on that point. But they also rampantly implored you to expect the unexpected. To be flexible. To be on the lookout for unplanned opportunities.

They were all, "Don't push the river," meaning go with the flow. And "If you get a lemon, make lemonade." Which is like if your life or your car or some other major purchase totally reeks, turn it into something good—like an excellent lawsuit, probably.

I was so glad I'd boned up on these things. Because when Josh plopped himself down between Lauren and me, and we were all comfy in the den and ready to view Brad's award-winning docudrama, one of those unexpected happenings broke loose.

I was wielding the VCR remote. I wasn't paying all

that much attention to it either because, face it, hitting the Play button is not one of your SAT requirements. From a fuzzy distance, I might have heard Dionne's voice. But I was all up in my head. Way more focused on what I would say to Lauren during and after the movie than on what was actually happening on the TV screen.

"Oh, no," I suddenly heard Lauren say. "I can't believe I brought the wrong tape. That's Brad, but this isn't *Moviemaker*. At least it's not the version I know. Oh boy, I hope I didn't mess up big time and bring some unfinished new piece he's putting together."

Then there it was again, De's voice. In loud and clear Sensurround. "I want to say, Brad, that I absolutely appreciate your confidence in me. You must be brutally gone on this Betty to part with these excellent locks."

I blinked at Lauren. Her choppy-cut auburn hair bounced in sympathetic confusion as she shook her head. "Could the cassette have been mislabeled?" she mumbled, staring at the TV screen.

"Yo, you got courage. Nerves of steel, bro," Murray's laughing voice was saying. "You wouldn't catch me putting my do in the hands of a raw amateur."

De's reply was predictably huffy. "It is not courage, it's commitment. That's the difference between mature love and some high school people's childishly simplistic ideas of being true blue."

"Can you believe it? What a dope. Leave it to me to pick up the wrong tape." Lauren was busy finding new ways to blame herself for the mixup.

But Josh knew better. As I turned toward the TV, he whispered, "Oh, no. I forgot."

Forgot what? For a minute I didn't understand what Josh was talking about. Onscreen, Brad was sitting at the dressing table in my room, getting his hair cut. This was definitely not *Moviemaker* we were watching. It was Tony's video version of today's makeover.

I looked around. Suddenly I saw the cassette Lauren had brought. There it was, sitting beside the telephone on the oak table right next to me, a rectangular black box labeled "Dietz/Moviemaker/20 min."

All at once I knew what had gone wrong. Brad and Moira had left their makeover tape in the VCR. And Josh had forgotten to put the cassette of *Moviemaker* in!

I turned to Josh for confirmation. "You never put that tape I gave you into the VCR, is that what you're telling me?" I whispered.

He nodded apologetically. "I was just going to make a fast call to Mom first. But I got caught up in the conversation, and then Harold got on the phone and decided to play dad—"

"And now we're watching Brad's makeover," I finished for him.

When all else fails, fast-forward. I did. And there was Brad, looking years younger, his Banderas hair magically Keanu-ed and flopping handsomely over his forehead. "Think she'll like it?" he was asking someone offscreen.

"If my instincts about Lauren are right—" a familiar voice answered.

"Cher, was that you?" Lauren asked. "I am so confused. Did you just say 'Lauren'?"

I fast-forwarded—fast.

"Okay, so I think I know what happened here," I said, trying to totally radiate positive energy in my smile. "It's one of those, you know, like 'If you get a lemon, make lemonade' kind of opportunities."

"Yes?" Lauren seemed to want more details.

"Oh, look at that," I enthused. It was Brad, helmeted and knee-padded, arms awkwardly out-stretched, wobbling beside Travis on his first skate-board run.

Lauren burst into laughter. "What's he doing?" She snorted between giggles. "He's going to kill himself."

Onscreen, Brad sailed toward the camera, scream-ing, "If this doesn't impress her, I give up."

"Who's he trying to impress?" Lauren asked.

Josh opened his mouth to respond. I brutally pinched his arm.

"Whoops, my bad," I said as he turned angrily toward me. "Hello, let's not get all Madonna–Sean Penn over this. It was just an accident, okay?" I protested. "Okay, so, here's my revised plan. First off, Lauren, you did not bring the wrong tape. You have not committed blunder one. What we are watching is a totally different video, one that was inadvertently left in my VCR. And if you'll just give me a trust-based minute, I think you'll find it even more excellentissimo than *Moviemaker*. Although I'm sure that one is Academy quality."

I hit the Fast-forward button yet again, cruising through makeover events. Every now and then I'd pause, just to let Lauren sample what her man had put himself through for her. We caught snippets of the poolside dance epic and Tai's cultural orientation session—which introduced Brad to vital pop icons from the Simpsons to Ren and Stimpy—and the clothing-the-feet ceremony, where Murray selected the perfect pair of chenille crew socks to complete Brad's sartorial conversion.

Finally, I found the moment I'd been searching for. Moira had videotaped it shortly after my makeover crew had left and just before I started showing Brad the Josh tapes. The three of us had been taking a break in the den. "You think this'll work?" Brad was asking me.

I hit the Pause button. Brad's handsome, newly clean-shaven face filled the screen. His dark eyes, caught in a touching moment of self-doubt, were especially appealing.

"Okay, Lauren," I said. "I sincerely hope you're going to like what we're about to view here. I have to say that I am holding some tension about this. Nothing extreme. Like I'm not leaking spinal fluid or breaking out in hives or anything. It's just a petite discomfort," I assured her. "The thing of it is, I, too, am brutally instinctive about romance. My match-making skills are legendary—right, Josh?"

"Uncanny," he agreed, beaming at me supportively.

"So, let me just clarify something before I hit Play. Lauren, arrogance and tacky accessories aside, do you find Brad Dietz attractive?"

"Of course I do," she answered. And her face

turned this revealing rosy hue. "But what's that got to do—"

"I knew it, I knew it, I knew it!" I pounded Josh's arm until he grabbed my hands and kissed them. Then I cleared my throat and called, "Okay, quiet on the set. Ready, three, two, one . . . and we are *rolling!*"

I thumbed the remote out of Pause and onto Play.

"I don't care whether my hair ever grows back or my pierced ear closes up forever. But is this going to do the trick?" Brad was asking me. "You don't really know Lauren, Cher. She's so bright and sensitive. . . . Is she going to fall for superficial changes?" His face clouded over. Then: "Listen to me," he said, breaking into an irresistible grin. "How desperate do I sound? But I love her, Cher. I don't know how to explain it. She's just . . ." Here Brad executed a totally adorable shrug. "She's, you know . . . Lauren."

You could hear Moira chuckling offscreen. Brad turned toward her, full face toward the camera, and Moira swept in for a close-up. "Lauren," Brad hollered. His face filled the screen. "I love you!"

Lauren's jaw dropped.

I clicked off the tape.

"Hey, wait," Josh said, wrestling me for the remote. "You left off the best part. You know, where you're telling Brad how to be just like me."

Suddenly Lauren stood up. "Oh boy!" She rolled her eyes. "How dumb. He didn't mean me, right? For a second I thought . . . Oh, gosh, how embarrassing. Listen, I've got to go."

"He did, Lauren. You are exactly who he meant.

143

Girlfriend, Brad Dietz is majorly gone on you. Sprung big time. He underwent one of the most formidable makeovers in which I have ever participated—all for you."

I looked at my watch. It was nine forty-five. The doorbell chimed, right on cue.

"I'll get it," Josh said, starting slowly to his feet. I grabbed his arm and yanked him back. "Sit," I commanded. "Er, Lauren, could you get that, please? I've got to . . . rewind."

She moved out of the room like a sleepwalker, shaking her head.

"It's Brad, isn't it?" Josh asked me. "Brad's at the door, right?"

"You are so smart! That's exactly who it is," I said, falling back onto the sofa beside him. I snuggled my cheek up against his denim shirtfront. "Josh, I've missed you so much," I said. "It's so excellent to have you back."

Chapter 19

*T*he victory party was Harriet Goddard's idea. Before Lauren had finished editing the final cut of Brad's new film, *Makeover,* Harriet decided to throw a bender for the cast and crew. She got Daddy to co-host, and Paramount Pictures to provide this excellent private screening room with totally plush upholstered swivel chairs and matching electric blue carpeting.

Daddy put the klieg lights on his Amex. Brad sprang for the fleet of limousines.

The buzz on his new opus was awesome. The whole town was talking about *Makeover.* The trade papers *Variety* and *The Hollywood Reporter* had turned Brad's name into a verb. To "Dietz" now meant to change, transform, or evolve. Like when MTV decided to spruce up its image, *Variety* reported that the music channel was "doing a Dietz."

De and I did a major Dietz ourselves, prepping for the party with an Olympic spree at the Beverly Center. By the end of the day our credit cards were limp. Among other trophies, De came away with a curvaceous white Herve Leger strapless number. I went all big-shouldered Thierry Mugler black. Daddy was so content to have Josh back that he barely commented on the profusion of shopping bags I shlepped past his door. And with an absolute minimum of wheedling, I got him to agree that I could enjoy one last fling on my towering Manolos.

Just to check my impulse, however, I faxed Christian a Polaroid of the strappy high heels. He phoned back immediate approval. "But only if you wear them with the Mugler," he instructed. "No briefcases, leatherbound day planners, or purple lipstick, promise? I've gotten reports on that power-dressing look you tried to pull off. Don't even think of it, girlfriend."

"As if," I complained. "Christian, that is so last week. I'm like evolved way beyond that. I mean, it's not like I think proactive is just a decent name for a deodorant, but I have moved on. Oh, boyfriend, I wish you could be at this bash. It's going to be so fun."

"Strap on those Manolo Blahniks and click your heels three times. You never know, right?"

"We'd probably wind up in Kansas."

"Save me a seat, anyway. I'm always with you, Cher, whether you can see me or not."

"Love you, boyfriend," I said.

How sentimental am I. The night of the *Makeover* screening, I tucked into my sequined evening bag this weird neckerchief Christian had bought me. He'd found it at one of his favorite antique clothing haunts. It had all these pre-Cuisinart household appliances, like eggbeaters and flapjack flippers, all over it in these squalid HoJo colors. I definitely intended to drape it over a screening room seat in honor of Christian.

"You look ravishing," Harriet commented as I descended the stairs. "Don't you think so, Mel? She's the picture of inner-directed, value-centered confidence."

Daddy, in a handsome dinner jacket, and Josh, in a more casually stylish ensemble, were staring up at me. "I don't know about all that," Daddy said. "She still looks a little too grown up for my taste. That dress is so . . . dark."

"Daddy, black is an extremely viable color," I said.

"And those shoes . . ." He shrugged his shoulders and sighed.

"You totally hate them?"

Daddy's furry eyebrows shot up. "Hate? Could I ever hate anything about you, Cher? On you even those miserable shoes look good. But . . . What are you doing?"

What I was doing was unstrapping my Manolos.

"Toss them here," Josh said.

I did, and he tucked them into his jacket pockets, then reached out his arms for me. With a very ungrownup whoop, I jumped from the stairs into Josh's arms. Daddy grabbed his heart.

"You're a nice kid, Josh. I'm very fond of you. But if you'd dropped her, well, I got a client from Las Vegas could make you disappear like *that*." He snapped his fingers. "And who'd miss you?"

"Gee, Mel. Who?"

Daddy patted Josh's cheek. "Me. You're so smart. Me, that's who. But don't you leave town again without consulting me, got it?"

The doorbell chimed.

"That'll be Brad and Lauren with our car," Harriet said. "We'd better go."

I tightened my arms around Josh's warm, cK one-scented neck, and he carried me out to the waiting limo.

The lights crisscrossing the sky outside Paramount's Hollywood studio were furiously festive. An excited crowd had gathered. As our cars approached the studio gates, Travis couldn't resist sticking his head through the moon roof of the long white limousine he was sharing with Tai, Elton, Amber, Janet, and Ringo. I saw him up ahead of us, pumping his fist and waving his skateboard at the fans.

"Who's that scraggly-haired lowlife?" Daddy wanted to know.

"That's Travis Birkenstock," Brad replied.

"The laid-back guru of the skateboard art," I said, quoting Moira. "He's Tai's boyfriend."

"Why am I not surprised?" Daddy grumbled as Travis scrambled onto the limo's roof and mounted his board.

"Wait until you see him in the movie," Lauren said. "You'll love him."

"Not unless Charlton Heston is playing his part. But I like the way you're dressed," Daddy said pointedly. "You see how this young woman is dressed, Cher?"

Lauren was in a little pastel pink sweater dress with a hairband holding back her wild auburn hair. "Thanks, Mr. Horowitz," she said. "Brad likes it, too. He calls it my Cher look."

"What focus, what concentration!" Harriet Goddard was staring through the window at Travis. Suddenly she signaled the driver to open the skylight in our car. He did, and Harriet clambered up onto the seat between Josh and me and stuck her perfectly coiffed head and excellently attired torso through the roof. Josh and I exchanged looks, then climbed up beside her.

The minute our heads hit daylight, the black stretch limo behind us started sounding its horn. We turned in time to see Murray and Dionne pop through their roof. "Cher, look who's here!" De hollered.

A grinning guy in a yellow leather dinner jacket surfaced between De and Murray. "Uh-oh, Toto," he called to me. "I don't think we're in Kansas anymore!"

"Christian!" I shrieked.

A loud crunching thud drew my attention back to the white car ahead of us. Travis had just catapulted off the roof and spun down onto the limousine's hood. The crowd went wild.

Harriet Goddard was riveted. Holding back a strand of hair that was flailing in the gentle breeze, she studied Travis, awestruck. "Creative, courageous, committed," she called down to my father. "That boy is executive material."

"Looks more like navel lint," Daddy growled up at us.

The klieg lights arced back and forth overhead. The Paramount gates, with their classic mountain logo, rolled open. The street crowd roared. And, waving to our fans and each other, we drove into the awesome studio to watch ourselves on the big screen.

Makeover was so fun, although it opened with this serious quote that went:

> Progress is impossible without change; and those who cannot change their minds cannot change anything.
> —George Bernard Shaw

When that flashed on the screen, we all went, "Whooaa, deep." After that it was a total commercial for being young, rich, and popular.

We watched ourselves cavorting in thrilling Technicolor, like rock groups that split up in the seventies. Every time one of us came on the screen, like everybody in the audience shrieked out the person's name. It was so empowering. And Brad tacked on this excellent sequence near the end, where he fast-forwarded through his own transformation. You could see him going from ponytail to center-part, stubbled chin to squeaky clean, gold jewelry to naked ear, wrists, and neck. It ended with that scene of him screaming into the camera, "Lauren, I love you!"

We whistled and stamped and applauded with major abandon. Then came the credits. We yelled even louder as our names appeared alphabetically. Finally, it said, "A Goddard Production," then, "Directed by Bradley Dietz." Then the screen went totally black. But the lights in the screening room didn't come back on. And we were all like, what is this? What's happening now? And all of a sudden, this message appeared in a tasteful white script across the black screen:

This film is dedicated to Cher Horowitz, who changed her mind and my life.

About the Author

H. B. Gilmour is the author of the bestselling novelizations *Clueless* and *Pretty in Pink*, as well as *Clueless™: Cher's Guide to . . . Whatever; Clarissa Explains It All: Boys;* the well-reviewed young-adult novel *Ask Me If I Care;* and more than fifteen other books for adults and young people.